About the editors:

Alison Campbell is co-editor
children and lives in London. She works with children and young
adults.

Caroline Hallett is co-editor of this and the previous two seasonal
collections. She works with young people in North London and
lives with her partner and young children just north of London. She
writes mainly on the train between work and home and is
travelling, hopefully, towards a collection of her own stories.

Jenny Palmer teaches EAP to postgraduate students at King's and
Goldsmiths' colleges. She has been writing and publishing since
1985, both journalistic and creative work. She lives in Hackney, but
is proud of and draws inspiration from her Northern upbringing.
She is currently researching and working on her third novel about a
witch, who she likes to think of as a long-lost ancestor. She is a
founder member of the collective who put together *The Man Who
Loved Presents* and *The Plot Against Mary*, and co-editor of this
anthology.

Marijke Woolsey has produced three novels, the first was short-
listed for the Betty Trask Award, and the third is with her agent.
She has also produced many short stories, some of which have been
published. She has two children. She teaches creative writing at a
Hammersmith and Fulham Adult Education College. She is co-
editor of *The Man Who Loved Presents*, *The Plot Against Mary* and this
anthology.

Also edited by Alison Campbell, Caroline Hallett, Jenny Palmer and Marijke Woolsey from The Women's Press:

The Man Who Loved Presents: seasonal stories (1991)
The Plot Against Mary: more seasonal stories (1992)

...And a Happy New Year!

more seasonal stories

EDITED BY ALISON CAMPBELL,
CAROLINE HALLETT,
JENNY PALMER AND
MARIJKE WOOLSEY

First published by The Women's Press Ltd, 1993
A member of the Namara Group
34 Great Sutton Street, London EC1V 0DX

British Library Cataloguing-in-Publication Data
A catalogue record for this book is available from the British Library

ISBN 0 7043 4386 X

Typeset in Bembo by Contour Typesetters, Southall, London
Printed and bound in Great Britain by BPCC Paperbacks Ltd,
Aylesbury, Bucks

Foreword

Welcome to this third volume of seasonal stories, sequel to *The Plot Against Mary* and *The Man Who Loved Presents*! Here is a collection that we feel sure will entertain and amuse you over the festive season and into the year to come.

Journey with us into a terrifying paranoid future and back into a rural childhood in pre-war Britain. Hurtle to the hard-hitting edge in surrealistic Spain and the bleak streets of North London. Run amok through a comical Christmas song and escape into the humid undertow of tropical nights. Glimpse the surprising rites of a pagan in Croydon. Discover new writers and savour the familiar. We hope we've provided a stimulating break from the mayhem of Christmas.

Thanks to all the people who have supported us, and special thanks to Kathy Gale, our editor at The Women's Press.

Alison Campbell
Caroline Hallett
Jenny Palmer
Marijke Woolsey

Contents

My True Love Sent to Me

Daphne Schiller

Jenna was rehearsing for her wedding night, prancing around in her nightie, when the doorbell rang. She flung on her negligee and went to see who it was.

It was the postman, carrying a tree. A large white bird sat on his hat.

'Jenna Fortune?' he enquired.

'Yes.'

'Special Delivery. One pear tree and accompanying partridge.' He removed his hat and gave the partridge a shove. It crept away, looking indignant.

'For me?' asked Jenna.

'So it says,' replied the postman, waving a card. ' "To my beloved, the bird of my dreams. Long may you perch on my tree. Love and kisses, Alfredo." '

'Do you mind?' said Jenna. 'That message is private.'

'Sorry,' said the postman, looking at Jenna's negligee. 'Don't get your feathers ruffled.' He replaced his hat and sauntered off.

Jenna looked doubtfully at the bird, then carried the tree into her back garden. It would do wonders for the patio, she thought.

The next morning the postman reappeared. Jenna had been jogging in her skin-tight, Dayglo track suit.

'He must be keen on birds,' the postman said, handing her a cage. Two bedraggled doves crouched in opposite corners.

'How lovely,' said Jenna uncertainly, wiping picturesque sweat from her brow.

'Starting an aviary, are you?' asked the postman, handing her a card.

Jenna read, 'To my love. May we bill and coo like this faithful pair, mates for life. Your dearest Alfredo.'

'I'm not sure they're up to it,' said the postman.

Jenna flushed. 'I've told you before, not to read my correspondence.' She slammed the front door. The birds slid across the cage and collided, squawking and pecking at each other. Then they put their heads under their wings and subsided into apathy. Jenna put them in the living room. They would be inspiring symbols of her future union, she thought. She made a note to buy grain in the morning.

However – on the following day, she had just had her bath when the doorbell rang. She wrapped a king-size towel round her and slipped on her mules.

'Bonjour!' said the postman.

'What?'

'Ça va?' he asked, giving her a wicker basket containing three hens. 'French hens, see?'

'Er – merci,' said Jenna. 'Are they egg-laying?'

'Bien sûr,' said the postman. 'All hens lay eggs. You could start a small poultry unit.'

Jenna read the accompanying note. 'To my little red hen. Egg-cite me with your soft body. Love Alfredo.'

'You'll need a run for them,' said the postman. 'And a dovecote for those doves. Shall I come round this afternoon?'

'Are you a handyman?' asked Jenna, surprised.

'You could say that,' said the postman, modestly.

'All right,' said Jenna, pleased. She thought how generous it was of Alfredo to have given her these delightful creatures. She opened the basket and released them. They made fluttering jumps at the partridge, then ran indoors and pecked the turtle-doves. Jenna was quite breathless when she recaptured them and shut them inside her shed.

She consoled herself with thoughts of Alfredo. He was wealthy, she was sure of that. He had often referred to his country estate and teased her about her humble first-time buyer's townhouse. Jenna was looking forward to being Lady of the Manor.

After lunch she put on her Buckingham Palace Garden Party outfit, so it wouldn't feel strange on the day. When the bell rang, she opened the door with an elegant gloved hand.

'Blimey! Is it the Mad Hatter's Tea Party?' asked the postman.

Jenna looked at him from under the brim of her hat.

'Come in,' she said. 'Have you brought your tools?'

'Of course,' said the postman, looking quite undistinguished in anorak, jeans and trainers. 'Or my name's not Harry Proudfoot.'

Whistling cheerfully, he carried wood, wire netting and various boxes into Jenna's garden. He worked without complaint, measuring, sawing and hammering. By the end of the afternoon he had constructed a dovecote and fenced off a chicken-run.

'Now you can put them in,' he said.

This proved difficult, with the simple-minded doves sitting in the run and the hens making futile efforts to reach the dovecote. The partridge jealously wobbled about, getting in everyone's way. Jenna wiped her face with her veil.

'I hope there won't be any more birds,' she said, disloyally.

The following day Harry played a jaunty tune on the bell, then handed over four boxes.

'If they're alive, they must be small,' he said.

Jenna took them gingerly, not wishing to risk stains on her new *après-ski* gear. She opened one.

'It's full of straw.'

'Cockroaches?' suggested Harry, giving her the card. It read, 'To my darling. Four calling birds to make time fly. Until you are mine, with every stroke, Alfredo.'

Jenna delved deeper. 'Cuckoo clocks,' she announced. She carried them in. At every quarter the cuckoos hurtled out, screaming hysterically. They weren't synchronised and Jenna couldn't adjust the mechanisms. Raucous sounds filled the house.

Jenna slept badly. The next morning there was no post, but she hardly noticed. She brought a dress for Ascot and was modelling it at home when the noise started. Jenna put her fingers in her ears but the ringing persisted. She rushed out and bumped into Harry.

'Cuckoo!' he said. 'I've been ringing for ages.'

'I thought you were another bird,' said Jenna, rustling her silks in a distraught manner.

'I'm registered mail,' he said, handing her a padded envelope. 'You have to sign for it.'

Jenna signed Harry's document and took the envelope. She opened one of five small boxes. The postman whistled.

'He's pushed the boat out this time.'

Jenna eased a slender gold ring on to her finger, then put on the others and read 'To my dearest. Wear my rings and you'll move in the best circles. Alfredo.'

'A bit arrogant,' said Harry, looking over her shoulder.

'Who cares,' said Jenna crossly, twitching her frills and flashing her rings at his eyes. She wore them for the rest of the day, despite her desire to throttle the cuckoos with them.

After another disturbed night, she had just put on her Jane Fonda leotard when the bell rang.

'Back to the birds this time,' said Harry.

'Oh no!' said Jenna, confronted by six sturdy geese. 'There's nowhere to put them.' She untied the label from the neck of their leader.

'To my little goose. Let me feather your nest with my golden eggs. From your loving gander, Alfredo.'

'Mixed metaphors,' said Harry, disapprovingly. He watched as the geese hissed at the hens and cackled derisively at the doves. The partridge buried itself in its tree and played dead.

'I'll be round this evening to make them a run,' said Harry, patting Jenna on the shoulder.

After buying a dress for Henley, Jenna returned to find him at work. The geese were penned, but the cuckoos defeated him.

Jenna sighed. She looked at Alfredo's photograph, his neat moustache and glowering eyes. He hadn't proposed yet, but she was sure he would. Unfortunately he had been compelled to spend Christmas with an aged aunt, but had assured her he would think of her every day.

That night, as she drifted into an uncomfortable sleep, she almost hoped that she might, for once, slip his mind. But in the morning there was a terrible kerfuffle. Jenna crawled out in her mohair dressing gown.

'It's getting beyond a joke,' called Harry, nursing his right arm. 'These birds are more than I can handle.' Jenna saw seven powerful swans strutting around the garden like petty gangsters. Even the geese retreated to the far corner of their pen. The partridge, resigned to agoraphobia, peered palely from behind its curtain of foliage.

'If you expect me to dig a river for them,' said Harry, leaning weakly on the fence, 'I'm afraid you'll have to think again. One of them walloped me.'

'Oh dear,' said Jenna. 'I'm so sorry. Perhaps they could go in the bath.'

'Do whatever you like. I'm off.'

'Oh no!' said Jenna. 'How can I manage them on my own?'

'Call Alfredo,' snarled Harry, hurling a card at her.

Jenna read, 'To my swan princess. Long may you swim through the river of my dreams. Let's snuggle down together. Love, Alfredo.'

Tears came to Jenna's eyes as the swans jostled her rudely. She felt too tired for breakfast, so went back to bed and slept intermittently till lunch time. Still in her dressing gown, she fetched pen and paper.

'Dearest Alfie,' she began. 'I can't thank you enough for your lovely gifts. I am wearing your rings at the moment,' (she looked down and noticed a rash was spreading from her third finger) 'and the birds are doing well. Shall we eat a goose later this year? Or do you prefer swan? I hope you enjoyed Christmas with your aunt. Love Jenna.'

A cuckoo screeched and she realised she hadn't mentioned the clocks. I'll write again later, she thought.

The next morning she had revived sufficiently to have put on her designer jeans. A low moaning sound was followed by a confident knock. Jenna opened the door to a bevy of milkmaids, each with accompanying cow.

'Good morning, Ms Fortune,' a cheerful girl said. 'We are the eight maids-a-milking, sent by Alfredo Von Gugelmann. Here's his card.'

'Er – did you have to bring cows?' Jenna asked. 'And where's the postman?'

'Of course we have to bring cows,' the milkmaid replied, affronted. 'They're part of the package. Don't you want to read your card? It's frightfully witty.'

'Oh, that,' said Jenna. The cows were eating her shrubs as she read, 'To my little cow-eyed girl. You can milk me any time. Udder-stand? Love, Alfredo.' She thrust it into her pocket.

'The postman said to tell you he's off sick. Had his arm in a sling. Now, where can we do our business?'

'Oh, round the back,' said Jenna vaguely. She watched in a daze as the milkmaids shooed the cows into spare corners and set up their three-legged stools.

They sang merrily as they worked. After milking, they scrubbed the shed and wheeled in huge churns. Then they stirred and pounded with gusto.

'Is there anything you need?' asked Jenna, politely.

'Breakfast,' said their spokesmaid. 'Fruit juice, eggs, bacon, sausages, tomatoes, fried bread. And plenty of toast and coffee. That'll do nicely, thanks.'

Jenna paled. 'It may take a while,' she said faintly. It took a long time, as did the shopping for the milkmaids' lunches and suppers. Cooking and washing-up also occupied her as cows trampled past and milkmaids careered about with massive yokes, banging into the walls. They didn't stop until late at night when they camped out in the living room.

They were up again at six, but Jenna felt too depressed to stir. She had a headache and her fingers were swollen by the pressure of the new rings. The next thing she knew was that nine enthusiastic drummers were parading around her bed.

'Beat it!' Jenna yelled. At the foot of the bed was a note. 'To my own true love. At the thought of you, excitement beats in my heart. Let's reach a crescendo. Alfredo.'

Jenna sleepwalked through the day, wearing a motley collection of old clothes. The catering and noise were greatly increased. The following morning, ten pipers arrived. ('To my one and only. Let music be the food of love. Yours, in harmony, Alfredo.') He's not even original any more, thought Jenna.

When eleven lady folk-dancers came on the eleventh day, Jenna screamed loudly. Tripping awkwardly over the unsewn hem of her oldest trousers, she made for the gate.

'There's a card,' a lady called.

'I don't want it,' shouted Jenna, but the ladies smiled and surrounded her. In despair, Jenna read, 'To my lady. Come dance with me. Your partner, Alfredo.'

Jenna slumped over the front gate, her head in her hands. A tap on her shoulder roused her. She looked up to see Harry.

'I gather you've got visitors,' he said.

'Rather a lot,' said Jenna, wearily. 'I can't sleep and I'm worn out.'

'You do look tired,' Harry agreed. 'And your dress sense isn't what it was. Perhaps you need time off, like me.'

'I'm sorry,' said Jenna. 'How's your arm?'

'Mending. I'm back at work tomorrow.'

'I might see you then,' said Jenna, turning away regretfully. 'I have to write a letter now.'

She returned to the house and wrote:

Dear Alfredo,

    although grateful to you for your many gifts, I have to tell you that my little house can't accommodate any more. If you persist in sending me presents, I shall be forced to return them. Christmas is nearly over and it seems unnecessary and ostentatious to continue this performance. I hope your aunt is well.

    From Jenna.

Feeling better, she deposited the cuckoo clocks at the bottom of the garden. With the aid of an umbrella, she ejected three swans from the bathroom, then began the painful business of soaping her hands to ease off the rings. Having accomplished this, she made herself a large omelette.

'You can cook for yourselves today,' she told a piper. His bagpipes crumpled.

'Look after the birds, will you?' she asked an astonished milkmaid. 'I'm going out.'

In town she brought a full-skirted white dress with matching shoes and tights. After some dithering, she chose a hat with a drift of veil. When she returned, Jenna put her ear-plugs in and watched old films on television.

She slept that night with a clear head. In the morning she rose early and put on her new clothes. The doorbell rang. Harry was there with twelve lords who leapt over the threshold.

'Do you want his note?' Harry asked.

'Not really,' said Jenna.

'I'll read it anyway,' said Harry. 'I don't like waste. It says, "To my intended. My heart leaps when I think of you, Alfredo."'

'Well, my heart sinks when I think of you, Alfredo,' said Jenna, tearing the note to pieces.

'I see that your self-possession has returned,' said Harry, approvingly. 'And is that a wedding dress you're wearing?'

'It might be,' said Jenna, as the lords leapt round the garden. 'But that, of course, depends on you.'

'Couldn't we keep one of the hens?' asked Harry, as they departed.

'Not one,' said Jenna, firmly.

'Shall I propose by letter,' asked Harry. 'Would that be appropriate, do you think?'

'I've had quite enough letters recently,' said Jenna. 'But we'll write to Alfredo and propose he gets lost.'

So that was what they did.

Gastric Measures

Susan King

They told her it was all in her mind. For fourteen years, they told her, and she believed them. What else could she do?

The first doctor blamed her 'O' levels; the second, her 'A's; the third put it down to worry about boyfriends; the fourth? – she didn't have any children; the fifth? – she did. But whatever they told her, they didn't take the pain away. The pain that nagged at her insides, that was eating her stomach away, that would erupt like a volcano and send her reeling across the room, throwing her on to the floor gasping for breath. They did tests of course, for an ulcer, or a growth, but these revealed only one thing. There was nothing physically wrong with her. It's all in your mind, they said. Stop worrying, or you will end up with an ulcer, and then you'll really be in trouble. Have a holiday, take up yoga, go for long healthy walks. Just stop bothering us.

And so she learnt to keep the pain to herself. Or almost did. It was impossible to keep it from Donald. After all, she was married to him, and it's not easy to put pain attacks on a timer. They often came at night, catching her unawares. At first Donald had been sympathetic, brought her hot-water bottles, wiped her brow, called the doctor. Of course that was the end of it all. The doctor (number six) explained to him, in simple layman's terms, how it was all in her mind. A form of attention seeking, he offered as an explanation. A doctor destined for a great career in psychiatry.

Donald took away the hot-water bottle and told her to pull herself together. When she didn't, and insisted on having more pain attacks, he left her. Six months later she received a letter from his solicitor. She was unsuitable to be a mother, it told her, and Donald was claiming custody of the children.

'He hadn't got a chance,' everyone said. 'They never take the kids away from the mother. Don't worry or you'll make yourself ill.' Three weeks before the court case, a woman in a pink velour leisure suit holding a lead which ended at a Rottweiler knocked at the door. She declared herself to be Mandy and introduced the dog as 'Hercules'. She and 'Donny' were now living together, she told Susan. They had a lovely house with a garage with automatic doors. She just wanted to talk, like two girls together. So Susan would understand. She'd look after Peter and Lucy. She couldn't have kids herself, you see. She only had Hercules; he made a lovely pet but it wasn't the same. So Susan would let the kids go, wouldn't she? After all, she wasn't really capable of looking after them. Donny had told her all about Susan's problem. She could talk to her about it if she liked.

Her mother's friend had been in a mental hospital, so she understood these things. They could become friends.

Mandy never pressed charges, although she did report it to the solicitor, which didn't help Susan's case any. She probably had another dozen leisure suits anyway. The cat's litter tray had simply been the nearest thing to hand. For once Susan hadn't felt so guilty about forgetting to clean it out for so long.

She dreaded seeing them at court, but as it turned out she needn't have worried. The night before the case came up she went out with some girlfriends for a few drinks, to take her mind off it. On the way home she felt the pain start, and took a short-cut through the park to get home before it exploded. She didn't make it. She passed out under a forsythia in bloom. The babysitter, panicking when she wasn't home by midnight, called the police. They found her at three in the morning. 'Dead drunk,' the policeman wrote in his notebook. 'Not fit to look after the children,' was the verdict. Hercules got the children and Susan was sentenced to a lifetime of loneliness.

She got a job in a bookshop and for a while it helped. But then the pain came and she was sent home. Eventually she was sent home for good. 'You're upset about the divorce and losing the children,' said doctor number seven. 'Here take some tranquillizers and some sleeping pills. They might help.'

They did, when she took the whole bottle. She woke to the smells of hospital and the sound of voices whispering. 'She's got a history of nerves,' they said. 'It was only a matter of time . . . A matter of time,' said a different voice, aeons later, a woman's voice accompanied by the swish, swish of a mop. 'He said it was only a matter of time before I passed one, and if I did, it could get stuck and block a tube, and I'd be knocking on the gates of heaven.' 'Well I never,' said another voice, 'tut, tut, tut.' The mops swished in harmony. 'How many did you have?' . . . 'Thirteen all told. I was so glad to get rid of that pain. I'd had it for years. It used to knock me for six, it did. Felt like an 'and grenade had gone off in me stomach.' The swishing sounds moved away.

Susan sat up in bed. 'What was it?' she yelled. The patients and the two men in overalls stared at her. 'The pain,' she yelled, 'what was it?' She could see the nurses advancing upon her, syringes at the ready. 'For God's sake tell me, what was it?'

'Why gall stones dearie, said one of the mop holders, 'I had gall stones. But why do you want to know.'

'Strange,' said doctor number eight when the results of the test came through. 'I would never have thought it. Fat, female and fifty we always say, and you only qualify on one of those accounts.' He must have thought this was funny; he laughed enough.

She had the operation a month before Christmas. They threw away her gall bladder but kept the stones for her, as a souvenir. They put them in a jar, labelled it with her name, and put it on her bedside table. When she was well enough she picked it up and turned it round and round. They were quite pretty, a speckled brown, like tiny quails' eggs. She counted ten; exactly the right number.

She sat in her empty house listening to 'God Rest Ye Merry Gentlemen' on the radio with ten boxes of chocolate coated Brazil nuts in front of her. With the precision of a bomb disposal operator she peeled open the cellophane and slipped the boxes on to the coffee table. She lifted the lids and smiled at the rows of shining chocolate brown balls. From a kitchen which still smelt of melted chocolate, she took a plate of ten such balls and added one to each box. She was satisfied; there was no way you could tell the difference, not until you bit into them, that was.

She returned each box to its cellophane coat, added a layer of brightly coloured Christmas paper, and finished off with a top cover of brown. She picked up her pen and began to write. She sent one to each of the eight doctors who had been so kind to her all her life, with thanks from a grateful patient. She sent the other two to Donny and Mandy, 'with best wishes for Christmas and a Happy New Year.' It was a pity she only had ten. Poor Hercules would have to be left out.

. . . And A Happy New Year!

G A Pickin

'Don't just stand there staring at it, bring it in,' Janet ordered her sister. Hattie hesitated over the parcel on the front step a bit longer, her hands hovering above it in mid-air like some reluctant bird circling a decoy.

'It's been jiggled about in the delivery van all this time, it's hardly going to explode now.' Janet's tone implied an inept cowardice on Hattie's part, although Hattie noticed that her sister was not stepping forward to retrieve the parcel herself.

'There have been three deaths from parcel bombs this week, and only two of them were delivery men. They say that each group has their own device now, and different mechanisms respond to different triggers,' Hattie defended herself.

In the last eight months, it seemed that every faction of society with a grudge, both at home and abroad, had taken to sending the lethal packages through the post. At first it was restricted to the usual terrorist organisations with the predictable political targets. But with the successful elimination of six MPs, others decided to use the same methods.

Christmas, the festive gift-giving season, gave everyone the perfect cover for avenging their wrongs. They were aided and abetted by the more unscrupulous, sensation-seeking press, who printed enough details on the 'cunningly simply but fiendishly effective' devices, that only the most ignorant of illiterates could fail to concoct a working bomb. Pop stars, chat show hosts, virtually anyone in the public eye proved a legitimate target.

When it became clear that even personal grudges between neighbours, relatives and employees were being solved in this grisly manner, the Post Office refused to deliver anything larger than an A4 envelope, and that had to be completely flat. Musical Christmas cards with those tiny round batteries went straight to the bomb disposal squad. The country came to a standstill, and businesses suffered enormous losses. Charities, relying heavily on mail-order trade, declared bankruptcy.

The prime minister ordered the Post Office to resume parcel delivery, which brought about an all-out strike of recalcitrant postal workers. They had a point, for just over half the deaths so far had been amongst their numbers, not to mention casualties, all of whom would have to receive compensation.

All was not lost, however. This being a free market society, private companies stepped into the breach overnight, quite prepared to risk the danger and deliver anything, regardless of size, for a fee. The sight of helmeted, be-gloved figures cautiously removing tinsel-festooned packages from within steel-plated vans with specially reinforced grilled windows became commonplace in most districts.

Present choosing had become a nightmare, and wary parents had advised grandmas to send a cheque rather than risk the hideous consequences for the children. It is surprising how quickly people can become used to almost anything.

'Stop being a ninny!' Janet snapped. Hattie, her nervous fingers gingerly touching the brown-papered sides, turned her face away and lifted the shoebox-sized object up. Holding it out at arm's length, she placed it carefully on the dining room table.

'It's addressed to you, Hattie,' Janet said, disgruntled. 'I can't make out the postmark, though. It's all smudged. Since all deliveries went private, you can't even tell by the stamps where it might come from.' She pushed her glasses more firmly up her nose and leaned closer to the shiny brown surface.

'This bit looks like a "U" and "S". Sussex? Who do we know in Sussex?' Janet touched a manicured fingertip to the knotted twine in the centre of the package.

'Maybe it's from the United States,' Hattie said. 'I know we haven't heard from Auntie Sarah in years, but it's possible, I suppose. I can't think of any other "U" "S" that it could be.'

A frown brought unfamiliar wrinkles to the skin around Janet's eyes.

'Why would Auntie Sarah suddenly send a Christmas parcel to you, rather than to both of us?'

'I don't know. Perhaps she's died and left us something in her will, and my share has arrived first. After all, we're lucky to get any sort of post these days, with things the way they are.'

'There would have been a letter from the solicitors first, surely, checking our bona fides,' Janet said, placated slightly.

'We don't even know it *is* from America. It could be some clothes I sent for out of a catalogue months back, even as long ago as last year, and its only just arrived now. I'll bet it's a cardigan, something like that.'

Hattie weathered her sister's stormy look as best as she could. Janet would never be seen dead in clothes bought from a catalogue, even if they were a top designer's offerings (which Hattie's certainly were not).

'You simply can't tell how it will look on you, the colour, the cut, until you've tried it on,' Janet was always telling her. Even if you *did* resemble the model. Hattie had no illusions there.

Janet, with her still-girlish figure, had married money, and had long since forgotten what it was like to count pennies. When her husband died she had graciously opened her home to Hattie, but after several years, Hattie still felt like an awkward visitor, clumsy amidst the fine china and dainty furniture. This feeling intensified at this time of the year as the house filled with porcelain angels, delicate baubles and precarious ivy garlands.

'Well, don't keep us in suspense, Hattie. Open it up!'

The two sisters faced each other across the top of the package. Janet's face was eager, encouraging, while Hattie's was troubled. She deepened her frown still further as she spoke.

'I don't know. It might not be safe. It's not as if I was expecting a parcel.' Hattie sighed. 'Not even at Christmas time.'

Janet snorted in exasperation. 'Don't be silly. You said yourself it was probably some new cardigan out of the catalogue. Or what if it *is* from America! Imagine, Auntie Sarah remembering you after all these years. You did used to spend Christmas with her in the old days down in Dorset, which I never did.'

Hattie recalled the excruciating days of feigned politeness as she listened to the woman, old even then, droning on and on about Christmases spent as a girl on the farm in Devon, relating pointless tales which involved who had given what gift to whom, and how much each gift had cost. The rewards for this endurance were a glow of self-righteousness from an unpleasant but necessary chore performed, and an enormous turkey dinner with all the trimmings, which more than made up for the rest of the month's meagre rations. It had been a relief when the old bat had emigrated to the warmer climes of Arizona, a parting that brought more rumbles from the stomach than tears from the eyes.

'Perhaps she was looking through some old photographs and suddenly got the urge to get in touch again. You know how old people turn to their past more and more to escape from their tired, endless present, especially at this time of the year.' Janet was caught up in the romance of her own tale.

'I wish there was some way to know for certain,' Hattie said. 'Wasn't there a set of guidelines the government issued on how to approach suspect packages? I remember putting the paper to one side so that I could cut that bit out and save it, just in case, but I don't think I ever got round to it.' Hattie half-heartedly turned this way and that, looking round the be-tinseled room for an old newspaper that would long since have been used to lay the fire.

She wiped her sweaty palms on the skirt of her dress.

'I think one of the precautions is to immerse the parcel in water for 30 minutes,' she said. 'That wouldn't harm a cardigan. I never get wool, makes me feel itchy all over.'

'But what if Auntie Sarah's sent you some family documents, old photos, priceless keepsakes?' Janet clasped Hattie's arm. 'They'd be ruined forever, and all because of a groundless fear. Be sensible, for goodness' sake! Who on earth would want to send you a parcel bomb? You haven't an enemy in the world.'

Hattie prised her sister's fingers off her arm and squeezed them gently before letting them go. She crossed to the dresser and switched on the radio, and 'God Rest Ye Merry Gentlemen' filled the room.

'You never know who you may have offended in the past, what unintended slight or snub may have sent someone to brooding. These days, even an act of charity can give rise to the resentment.' She looked Janet in the eyes. 'Even hatred.'

'. . . to save us all from Satan's power . . .' the radio sang.

Janet squirmed uncomfortably under this scrutiny, but shook it off and smiled.

'I'm sure no one could ever hate you, Hattie,' she said warmly.

Hattie turned her back on her sister and mumbled something that Janet did not quite catch.

'Pardon?'

Hattie paused before replying, and the choir wished them '. . . tidings of comfort and joy.'

'I'm going to ring the police. They'll surely have some experts they can send, people who can advise us properly about what to do.' She headed towards the door of the lounge.

'Wait,' Janet called. 'They can't possibly send out a bomb expert to everyone who receives a parcel. I'm sure that sort of treatment is reserved only for politicians, important people. Even if they *do* have someone doing the rounds for us ordinary mortals, there's bound to be a waiting list. It might be weeks before they get round to us, and I'd just die of curiosity having to wait that long.'

Hattie gave Janet a peculiar, pitying look.

'Nonsense,' she said. 'Better a bit of suspense than having your hands blown off for want a little patience. Surely you could stand to wait a few days.' Hattie could remember how Janet as a child had always peeped at their presents, hidden in their parents wardrobe, and spoiled her surprise by telling her what they all were.

Janet became more insistent, 'What if they do one of those controlled explosions, take it out in the middle of a field somewhere and blow it up. Then we'd never know what was in it, or even who it was from.' She caught at Hattie's arm again, this time more firmly. 'Let's take a chance and open it.'

Hattie looked down at her sister's whitened knuckles as they bunched the material of her sleeve.

'. . . news of great joy, news of great mirth . . .' the radio sang. 'You're hurting me.'

Janet withdrew her hand, started to speak, and then, thinking better of it, simply shook her head slowly instead. Hattie turned without another word and marched through to the lounge. She picked up the telephone receiver and punched in a number, then waited, holding the receiver away from her ear. She cocked her head towards the dining room door, listening.

A familiar sound rewarded her, the sideboard door opening and closing, its brass handle tapping the wood as it swung. There was a faint snip of scissors as they cut through the twine, then a delicate rustle of paper gently pulled aside. There was a pause, and then the crack of stapled cardboard as the box was prised open. At the same time, the carol from the radio ended.

For a long moment, complete silence filled the house the two sisters shared. Then came the deafening, horrific explosion. The dust settled, and there was silence once more, except for a soothing tone coming from the telephone receiver, which, up until now, had gone unheeded. A new song spilled brightly from the radio.

'On Christmas night all Christians sing . . .'

Hattie lifted the telephone to her ear now, and listened to the pleasant voice of the speaking clock telling her it was ten forty-seven and thirty seconds. Replacing the instrument in its cradle, she crossed the room to the door.

' 'Tis the season to be jolly . . .', sang the choir. She looked in only long enough to confirm that Janet was dead. It did not take more than a glance; the damage had been rather more severe than she had expected, and she had never been able to stand the sight of blood. She retraced her steps to the telephone and this time punched in 999.

While Hattie was waiting for the police to arrive, she opened the little drawer of the telephone table and pulled out the envelope that had come from America two days before. She reopened it now, no longer feeling guilty because it was addressed to her sister, and withdrew the copy of a will which Auntie Sarah's solicitor (or attorney, as they were called in America) had sent. She read again the relevant paragraph before replacing it in its drawer. The whole of Auntie Sarah's estate, which included a large sum of money in dollars and an apartment house complete with paying tenants, was divided equally between the two sisters, or the whole to the survivor, should one predecease the other.

Hattie was able to appear suitably distraught when the police arrived. They would never be able to determine who it was that had wanted to blow up Hattie. As Janet had said, no one could hate such a quiet, self-effacing person. And what possible motive could there be? She had only her state pension and a few premium bonds, all to be used for a nice funeral when she died. At least, that was all she had been worth when the parcel first arrived. Now, of course, things were quite, quite different.

The package would be traced to a Sussex delivery company, but the sender's name and address, as in so many other cases, would prove false, a dead end. The clerk who took the order might remember a rather non-descript female who paid cash, but it was more likely that the whole transaction would have merged with all the others that had seemed without incident or suspicion.

The kind policewoman comforted Hattie, telling her not to blame herself. It could not be her fault if Janet's insatiable curiosity had turned out to be fatal.

'If only she'd listened to me,' sobbed Hattie, 'she'd still be alive.'

'. . . the hopes and fears of all the years are met in thee tonight,' the radio comforted.

Picturebook

Jenny Palmer

The farm lay at the foot of Pendle Hill. Our family had lived in it for generations, going on 500 years, the same family handing it down through the centuries to their next of kin. My mother was the one to inherit it, the only one of five sisters interested in farming.

The house was a large stone building with mullion windows, like you got in weaver's cottages. It had been built to last. The windows looked out on to the garden at the back, which was actually the front, and then out towards Pendle. Inside the house, there were initials of previous occupants, scratched in the oak beams. Washing hung on a rack over the inglenook chimney breast, which rose up from an open range fire.

In former more austere times, the chimney had been open to the sky, but it had since been blocked off to keep out the cold North Easterly wind, which still whistled down the chimney at every opportunity, and sneaked in through nooks and crannies, and under the solid oak doors which were not designed to fit. It blew in down the lobby, and under your feet, and then out up the chimney again.

In winter we huddled together around the fire to keep warm, burning our legs until they were mottled at the front, but still feeling chilly at the back from the draught. We boiled water on a soot-blackened kettle on the open range.

'A cup of cocoa and then off to bed,' said my mother.

It was Christmas Eve. When we went to bed, we hung up our stockings, and I prayed that Father Christmas would remember me most, and fill my stocking to the brim. We had written our lists well in advance, and left them on the mantelpiece for Santa, when he came down the chimney. Every year I asked for a scooter. Perhaps he never got the letter. Or perhaps a scooter was too heavy to carry all the way from the frozen North. Sometimes I worried that he would get stuck in the chimney. We had an Aga and the flue was very narrow. One year the Aga had gone out on Christmas day. I thought it must have been Santa carrying my scooter down the chimney, but I got a watch that year so it couldn't have been. I gave up asking for a scooter after a while. It was obviously too difficult to carry.

It was also difficult getting to sleep and Father Christmas wouldn't come if you were awake. I took to counting sheep. Ninety-eight, ninety-nine. I didn't often get to the hundred. When I got bored, I looked at the ceiling. The light from the oil lamps danced around and made patterns on the oak beams. If I looked hard enough, I could see the face of the Queen. I could make out her profile quite clearly on the beam. My mother adored the Queen and wouldn't have a word said against her. Every night I searched out the Queen in the woodwork. If I could find her, I would have my mother's blessing, and could fall asleep.

I was awoken that night by the sound of footsteps steathily moving towards my bed. It must be Father Christmas already. I couldn't look. He would go away. I heard him lean down and leave a stocking, and then take away my old one. I kept my eyes tight shut, until I heard him walking away. Then fell asleep again.

Halfway through the night, I heard the rustling of paper from my sister's room, as she fumbled through her stocking, and her voice whispering excitedly.

'He's come,' she said. 'What did you get?'

I didn't say anything. I pretended to be asleep. My sister was born on Christmas Day. She always got two presents instead of one. I didn't want to know what she had got. Besides we didn't have electricity, so you couldn't see a thing. You had to use guesswork to discover what was in the stockings. There was always an apple, and an orange and then stocking fillers, wrapped in tissue paper, diaries and pens and pencils, sugar mice, chocolate drops and sometimes even a torch, which made the searching easier, if you could find the batteries. The stockings were my dad's old ones, darned at the heel and toe, ones he didn't wear any more.

I waited till morning to find out the contents of my stocking. It was the usual things, the fruit and sweets and all. But there was something else underneath the stocking. A huge big brown-paper parcel. I tore off the wrapping. It was a book entitled 'A Day in Fairyland'. No one else had such a book. Not even my sister.

The book was full of pictures of fairies and elves and pixies. And it was a giant book. Bigger than any I had ever seen. I reckoned I could slide down it in bed if I tried. I sat and pored over the book. The pixies and fairies were all involved in their daily activities in Fairyland. They lived in apparent harmony with each other and their surroundings.

Each character wore its own separate colour of clothes and seen together they all seemed to match as in a rainbow. Everyone was engaged in something. If they weren't collecting raindrops from the leaves and stems of flowers in tiny buckets, or painting tree trunks and collecting acorns in wheelbarrows, they were somer-saulting over clumps of grass and leap-frogging over toadstools, or conversing with squirrels and birds. Now I had a world which I could inhabit for hours at a time, and never feel bored. My favourite character was a maiden in a long green dress who sat by the side of the pool combing her golden locks and staring at her reflection. She had a little silver coronet on her head, and a magic wand in her hand.

I knew all about fairies since before I went to school. I knew about 'fairy hill' where the 'little folk' danced on certain nights of the year. I'd seen the magic stone circles where they danced. People still trudged to the top of Pendle to lay a stone on the beacon, just like they had always done. When anyone of us lost a tooth, it was the tooth fairy who came in the night and replaced it with a bright silver sixpenny piece.

But my mother's life was one of toil. She had developed a strict rota for her jobs. On Mondays she could be seen wrestling with the dolly tub doing the family washing. I struggled to help her swinging on the wheel of mangle. I couldn't budge it an inch. My mother was used to physical work. Tuesdays were for ironing with the flat iron warmed on the fire. Wednesdays were for shopping in Nelson. That took up the whole day. Thursday was for baking and Friday for cleaning. So it was and so it always had been.

Sometimes she tried to interest me in doing a chore for her. I didn't mind collecting the eggs or going round the sheep in lambing time, but when it came to washing-up and cleaning, I jibbed.

'Why?' I asked when she wanted me to do anything.

'Because' was her stock response. It was hardly enlightening. Then I did the jobs begrudgingly. Other times I escaped. Was that all there was to life? Work, work and more work?

On rainy days, we stayed indoors, getting under her feet.

'Why don't you paint something?' she suggested to keep us quiet. We got out the paints and sketch pads.

'What shall we paint?' we asked.

'A monkey up a gum-tree,' she said. But what did a monkey up a gum-tree look like? I had never seen one. So I drew the Queen instead, like she was on Coronation day with her crown on, and blue sash over her shoulder across her waist. I never tired of drawing the Queen.

Once I got my picturebook though, I wasn't short of something to paint. I copied scenes at home, and then tried to recreate them at school. That was more difficult. I had to rely on memory. With the stiff bristled paintbrush and powdered paints, I worked to my heart's content trying to recreate my fairy world. My paintings strewn with bristles which had somehow dislodged themselves from the brushes never quite achieved the effect I desired. The colours all seemed to run, so you couldn't tell who was who. I had to wait until I got home until I could conjure up the images again.

I hadn't liked school at the beginning. I hadn't spoken for the first six months. I hadn't been able to get the hang of lessons. Why did we have to sit still in rows in those black wooden desks? Why did we have to learn our times tables off by heart? Why did the ink spill out of the inkpots and blacken our fingers and then smudge our faces so that we came home filthy? Playtimes were even worse. Then boys charged around the school yard playing tag, and sometimes girls got into fights and started pulling each other's hair out.

After I got my picturebook, life changed. I started joining in more. I started talking and soon got the reputation of a chatterbox. Then I decided to join the Brownies. They met on Monday evenings after school. All day on a Monday I wore my brown uniform, complete with brown leather belt, adorned with a yellow tie around the neck, and finished off with a brown beret. I couldn't wait for the end of the school day.

Suddenly, the moment I had been waiting for came. Our class teacher from the 'Little Room', now Brown Owl, took down the red and white spotted toadstool from the top of the cupboard, on which it was kept the rest of the week, and placed it in the centre of the room. Brown Owl signalled us in to the magic circle from the four corners of the room. First the pixies, then the elves, then the fairies. We all joined hands and swirled around in a circle, our feet hardly touching the ground, until it was time to stop, breathless, and return to our corners. Once the initiation ceremony was over, it was followed with more mundane pursuits like building campfires, and lighting them by rubbing two sticks together, or practising First Aid on each other. But it was the dancing that I liked the best.

The next year I moved up into the 'Big Room'. It meant a change of teacher. Now we studied serious subjects like history and geography and scripture. We did joined-up writing, and heard all about the Greek and Nordic myths. We learnt to repeat the Lord's Prayer parrot fashion every morning, asking for our trespasses to be forgiven, and requesting our daily bread from God, who was a combination of Thor, the god of thunder, and Father Christmas, except he didn't bring you presents. He sat on his throne all day, up in heaven, with his long white beard trailing down in front of him, passing judgement.

At the end of the term, the school put on a Christmas concert for parents and villagers. I had been disappointed in previous years, at not getting a major role in Goldilocks or Cinderella. But finally my moment came. I was cast as the Swan Queen in a play probably made up by the teacher, since I could never afterwards remember the name of it. Dressed from head to foot in white, with a little silver coronet on my head, I swept on stage followed by a flock of dancing cygnets and delivered my lines faultlessly. I felt like the maiden in green from my picturebook. To crown it all, one of my fellow pupils sneaked a kiss on my neck, as I walked off stage.

It was the pinnacle of my glory, the peak of my success. Who knew where it would all lead? One day I might even be cast as Snow White or Sleeping Beauty. I saw my life stretched out before me, moving from success to success, the centre of my universe, instead of deferring to others. People would look to me now. I would be like the beacon on the top of Pendle. Shining for all to see.

That night, however, as I slept in my bed at home, I was shaken by a terrible nightmare.

'My picturebook has been torn in two!' I cried out. 'Someone has torn my picturebook in two.' My mother came running.

'Look,' she said, 'Here is your picturebook. No one has touched it.'

'It's no good,' I told her, 'It's torn and it can't be put back together again.' And no amount of comfort from her would make me change my mind.

Next morning I got up as normal, dressed and had breakfast, but before I caught the eight o'clock bus to school, I took the picturebook and hid it in a drawer at the bottom of the wardrobe.

Home for Christmas

Zhana

As long as she was in her mother's house, Brenda was to sleep in a separate bedroom, untouched by man. Lying in her childhood bed, she watched the shadows on the ceiling and imagined things that lived in the corners, things that had waited for her all year, waited for her to return. In the middle of the night, she stirred, to realise that a little girl stood before her in the remains of a dress which barely covered her, her hair hidden beneath a rag.

'Who are you?' Brenda demanded. 'What are you doing here?'

'I's Anna. Missy say I's not to have nothin' to eat all day today 'cause I's wicked.' She huddled her arms round her shoulders and looked around her. 'It's cold. Where we at?'

'My bedroom. Well, that is, my mum's house. What are you doing here? Where do you live?'

The child crumpled up and started to cry. 'I dunno where my Mama is. Massa done sold me 'way from her. Missy say I's her girl now and must do as she say. But she powerful mean. Whoo, that woman mean. And 'cause I dropped the big pot o' rice, she say I can't have nothin' to eat now for the rest of the day. Sure am hungry.'

She looked straight at Brenda with eyes almost too huge for the face that held them. The bones of her arms looked as if they would come straight through her dress, straight through the skin. As Brenda looked at this child, she recognised someone even more damaged and afraid, someone even more in need of looking after than she herself was. 'Come on, child. Let's get you something to eat,' she marched Anna down to the kitchen, opened the fridge door and hunted out some cheese and a loaf of bread. Best to feed her first, then decide what to do with her. 'You'd better wash your hands.'

'Yes, ma'am.' The girl looked about her in wonderment.

'Through there.' She pointed in the direction of the downstairs toilet, then set about cutting the cheese. Anna stood in the middle of the room, looking bewildered. 'Come on,' Brenda at last grabbed her by the arm, hoping she was not being too rough, led her to the sink and turned on the taps. 'Girl big as you is old enough to wash her own hands, child.'

'Yes'm.' Curiosity, fear and hunger all battled inside Anna, but hunger won. Her hands clean, she ran to the table and, grabbing the bread with one hand and the cheese with the other, shoved first one, then the other into her mouth.

'Don't eat so fast, child, you'll make yourself sick.'

'My mama always used to tell me that.'

'Where is your mother? What's her name?'

'She has big, soft hands and eyes that smile – sometimes.' Anna looked like she was about to cry again. 'The day they done took me away, she was tryin' not to cry, but I could tell she wanted to. I ain't seen her since.'

'Where is she now?'

'Missy say not to talk about her no more, else I'll get a beatin'.'

'No one's going to beat you anymore, child.' Brenda decided it was best to slip into a take-charge role. 'You're safe here. I guess you can stay overnight, anyway. It's Christmas, after all. In the morning, we'll have to . . .'

'Christmas, ma'am? Then it's my birthday, too. My mama says I was born on Christmas Day. That makes me eight years old today.'

'That's nice, Anna. Happy birthday.' Brenda didn't know what to believe and what not to. Feeling out of her depth, she decided to stick to practical things. 'You need a bath, child. And then bed.' Wrapped up in one of Brenda's old T-shirts, the child snuggled down with Brenda. Anna fell asleep the moment her head hit the pillow. The food in her belly gave her face a look of peace.

'I hardly ever get to see you anymore, now you're down in London.

I want my daughter home for Christmas, I said.' Monica's words on the telephone may have offered an invitation, but the voice had carried a command.

'I really don't want to go up there this year, you know,' Brenda tried to persuade Steve. Well, really, she hoped he would save her. Redeem her. Rescue her from having to make a decision, having to take a stand.

'Come on. It'll be fun. And it would make your mum really happy.'

'Oh, God. She won't be happy till she sees me at the altar. Or in my grave. Can't we just have our own Christmas? For once?'

But it was not to be. As the sun rose in the east and set in the west and rose again, so Brenda climbed into a train carriage, settled into a corner, taking up as little room as possible, her bag tucked into the overhead rack, Steve snuggled beside her, clasping her hand. And as the train's engine whizzed them along, Brenda hunched, scowling, in her seat, imagining the wheels gnashing beneath her, hoping to trap her legs, grind them up and spew them out. As usual, she had worried about losing the tickets, worried about missing the train or getting on to the wrong one by mistake. Visions of ending up in some tiny backwater, surrounded by white strangers, knowing no-one and no way out until after Boxing Day, haunted her. Although this was the place of her birth, she was a stranger here. This was not her home. She clasped Steve's hand a little tighter, and sighed. His white face, a passport through this alien land, moved close to plant a kiss on her cheek before diving behind his newspaper.

Although he still sat beside her, Brenda knew she was now alone and while her body continued on this track, her mind returned to its own journey. As the train bore her out of London, she began to relax as the movement hypnotised her, rocking her gently through the belly of England. The preoccupations of the week began to slip away from her. The journey wiped away thoughts of work, the office, her life, and settled, instead, on her dream holiday – a sunny, tropical beach. She was just peeling off her swimsuit when a cry ripped across the quiet, jerking her back into the train carriage. She jerked her head around to see a child's face, screwed up in agony, emit a piercing wail. 'Why doesn't his mother shut him up?' she silently snapped, her annoyance quelling any compassion she might have felt. Annoyance more at the answering cry which wailed in her own heart, the cry of a child longing to be heard. She clamped down her facial muscles to avoid shouting, 'Shut *up*!'.

The train did not have to think about where it was going, the route was laid out in two long, thin metal strips that climbed and fell and curved into Derby. And then the travellers crawled into a taxi and drove up to the row upon row of red brick houses, standing bright and cheerful as they awaited the coming of the Christ child.

'My baby's home at last!' Monica threw her arms around Brenda. She wanted to burst out crying, to cringe and pull away and run. Yet she wanted to stand there, with Monica holding her, always. The firmness of her mother's arms surrounded her as the December cold crept around her, pinching at her ears and her nose. And her mother's smell sat on her like the imprint of lipstick on her cheek, that perfume they always added to cheap cosmetics, mingled with the powder and the stuff Monica sprayed on her neck. Sat on her, identifying her, as clearly as the bright red mark on her cheek, so that anyone who smelled her would know that Monica counted her among her possessions. The older woman grabbed Steve's hands and stood back, beaming at him, 'At last.'

As Brenda and Steve crossed from the outside world into the home, Brenda felt she was crossing into a territory where anything could happen. The smell of Christmas assaulted their nostrils. A mixture of mincemeat and dumplings and spices and fruits soaked in rum, a mixture of anticipation, expectation and hope. A mixture of safety and helplessness. They'd arrived on Christmas Eve – as late as possible, Brenda had insisted. She was glad she had brought Steve. She could cling to him in this sea of nostalgia. As she passed through the door, she passed back into childhood. She was no longer a grown-up, no longer her own person. But Steve's being there reminded both her and her mother that she had a life of her own, a life in London that she was going back to.

Brenda settled mindlessly into the Christmas Eve routine. They helped her sister Deb set up the artificial tree, painstakingly fitting each branch into its colour-coded hole while Monica busied herself in the kitchen, preparing Christmas dinner. They decorated that tree within an inch of its life, until its tree-ness was no longer visible. Until it was a gleaming, glittering, glinting thing, its vaguely triangular shape dominating its corner of the sitting room.

Finally, Monica appeared. She inspected the tree, laden with garlands and ornaments in red, gold and green, balls, baubles, Father Christmases, plastic holly, miniature chocolate presents, Victorian hearts and Atalanta's golden apples, then declared, 'It needs more tinsel,' and trotted off to produce two more boxes. Steve had the task of stringing the lights, moving around and around the bulging tree while Deb and Brenda hoped it wouldn't fall over and prayed it wouldn't catch fire.

Christmas dinner was to be a huge turkey, the size of which was in no way influenced by the fact that there were only four people in the house. Monica marinated the turkey in spices for several hours before stuffing it and roasting it to a rich, golden brown.

The bird was served with two rices. One, the rice and peas, prepared the day before. Brown rice, boiled with a bit of onion, garlic, chili, and a bit of coconut cream, then mixed with gunga peas. Resting it for twenty-four hours allowed the subtle flavour of the coconut to come through. The other rice, a mixture of rice and wild rice, would be prepared on the day, fried with garlic and onion, then boiled in a mixture of water and juices from the chicken, with an added bay leaf.

This meal would be accompanied by a fresh green salad; fried dumplings, with crisp golden crusts and soft, fluffy centres; plantain fried in butter to a deep yellow. This feast was designed to last for several days and would be shared, along with generous helpings of rum punch and home-made fruit-cake, among the various friends and relations who dropped round to help celebrate the festive season.

Monica frequently interrupted her preparations to inspect the decorations, before finally giving her approval, as she handed the star to Steve. As he stretched up to place it on top of the tree, she clucked, 'It's a long time since a man did that.' As they plugged in the monstrosity, the little lights beamed out their glow with all their might, filling the corner with a red and yellow hue that made Brenda, for the first time, feel glad to be home.

At half-past seven, the four of them trooped off to the church, Monica struggling not to grin with pride as her family filed into the pew. Brenda stared up at the hundreds of flickering candles filling the church with their light. Why? Why here, surrounded by my loved ones, do I feel so alone? Dozens of familiar faces greeted her. 'Hello, girl. Long time no see.' 'When you comin' back home?' Brenda felt embarrassed. She was glad, though, that everyone made Steve welcome.

As the hymns floated up to the roof beams and beyond on the voices of the congregation, Brenda's heart began to soar with them, dancing and floating on the thought of the new-born babe, come to save the world. Then suddenly, slicing through the middle of her joy, came a sadness, an uncontrollable sorrow. And she wondered, 'Why am I feeling this way? Why am I so sad? Here I am, in the bosom of my family, safe and warm and loved. Whose Christmas am I remembering?' And there came from within her a deep anguish, a pain and a longing, a searing memory. She thought of all the people who couldn't be there that night, safe, warm and loved, who didn't have homes to go back to, homes filled with the smells of Christmas.

In the morning, when Brenda awoke, the coldness of empty sheets and pillows that had not been slept in stared at her from the other side of the bed. Hearing her mother rustling up the Christmas breakfast, she tore downstairs to the kitchen.

'Mum, have you seen that child?'

'Happy Christmas to you too, sweetheart.'

'Merry Christmas, mum. There was a child here last night, a dirty, raggedy little girl . . .'

Monica's fingers, dusted in pale white flour, stopped kneading the dough which pressed between them. She turned to stare at Brenda. 'Anna.'

'You knew?'

Monica slowly walked over to the table and sat down, motioning Brenda to do likewise.

'Isn't that funny. I'd almost forgotten. Before you were born, every Christmas Eve, a little girl would come to my bed. She'd always ask me if I knew where her mama was.'

'You never told me.'

'Well, after you were born, it stopped.'

'Really?'

'And I didn't exactly go around talking about it.'

'Who is she, Mama?'

'It was her eighth birthday.'

'Yes.' Brenda felt a chill go up her spine and suddenly wanted to change the subject. Monica ended the conversation by getting up and returning to her cooking. They didn't speak of it again.

Before the Snow

Helen Dunmore

She looks him dead in the eye. 'There – are – no – more – batteries,' she repeats.

His face wrinkles. 'But you *said*! You said you'd bought batteries and all. You *told* us we had to write down everything we wanted on our lists and I did, I made a list and it had batteries on it because I knew I'd need them if I got a Gameboy and –'

'I did buy batteries,' she cuts in, 'They're all used up. You used them all. None of us knew how quick that Gameboy would go through batteries. You can plug it into the mains, can't you?'

He stands in front of her, wrinkled and reddening. It is two p.m. and they have had the stockings, the presents under the tree, drinks before dinner, the dinner. When he crashed into the kitchen for his batteries Paula was putting away the blue and white pudding dishes she'd brought to the cottage all the way from the city so they could have their exotic fruit salad off the china they always used at Christmas. Lychees, passion fruit, kumquats, starfruit, tangerines with waxy leaves on their stems, glowing slices of mango lapping pineapple on the white platter her mother had left her. She brought the fruit from the city, too, padded in tissue and wrapped in brown paper bags so it wouldn't ripen too fast. Let other families gorge on heavy puddings.

'It's a *Gameboy*,' Kay whinges, 'My *Sega* plugs into the mains. I don't want to plug my *Gameboy* –'

Eric must have caught what Kay was saying. Paula heard his feet quick-padding overhead, up to the bedroom. Now he comes back and stands dramatically in the kitchen doorway, hands behind his back. He smiles.

'Here's Father Christmas,' he says.

The boy's face changes. It's all going to start again. Presents and paper and tearing and finding and having and batteries and –
'That's it now kids, you've had all your presents for this year,' Paula said at midday, when he and Maudie finished scouring under the tree. But she was wrong. Kay shoots her a look, then begins to clamour round his father.

'Dad, what is it, what've you got, Dad –'

'Hey, hey, steady now. Thought I heard someone asking about batteries,' and over his son's head, to his wife, 'I guessed this would happen. Those things eat up juice.' He brings his hands from behind his back and there it is, a white box with a transparent top and four fat cylinders nestled in it.

'Wow, Dad! A battery charger. Wow, c'n I –'

'Yeah. Now careful son, it's all fixed up. I been charging these batteries since last night.'

Paula watches their two heads duck over the plastic box. Her boy is shining now.

'Now mind,' warns the father, 'It's for Maudie too.'

'Maudie hasn't even got a Gameboy.'

'She has her Walkman,' says Paula.

'That uses different batteries,' slaps back Kay.

'Where *is* Maudie?' asks Eric, and they look round, and listen. Paula goes to the living room and there is Maudie, curled in a chair, thumb jammed in her mouth, staring not at the video which is running through for the second time but at the white space of the window. She's OK. Paula returns to the kitchen. The Gameboy winks, back in command.

'Will you take that thing out of here,' she says.

'You gave it to me,' mutters Kay.

'Come on son, come on upstairs and I'll give you a game. Your mother's tired.'

Paula kicks a tired piece of wrapping paper under the table. Batteries. She lets her arms flop on the table, and her head go down. The children hate to see her like this. Two-seventeen on Christmas afternoon.

If it was a proper winter they'd be outdoors, skiing. Pack the children into their snowsuits until they're as fat as bears. Get the four pair of skis from the shed and go out into the cold blue afternoon, over Silverhill and down to the flats where it was easy skiing for the kids. But there's no skiing this year. Night after night the ground freezes. It is black and hard, a foot deep. Bushes lean skinnily against the wind, dying. They will die without the comfort of snow. On TV they show birds dropping through the pall of frost, dead on the wing. One day parents were warned to keep home their children under ten. Even in the city Paula kept Kay and Maudie home, warmed by the steady breath of central heating, while dossers collapsed in the iron-hard park. Paula's breath froze on her lips. Her nose ran and the snot made curls of frost.

But there was no snow. The sky was hard and cloudless by day. By night it was jabbed by icy stars and a thin wind turned overcoats to cotton. The climate's changing, people said, as they looked for the snow.

Paula stares out of the kitchen window. There is no wind now, only a quiet shudder of cold in the pine branches. It is grey, a close, tight-knit grey. Is it warmer? Will the sky yellow and thicken and send down the snow? She goes to the window and squints at the outdoor thermometer. It is a couple of degrees warmer. If the temperature went up a few more degrees they might have snow. She hears Kay babbling to Maudie in the living room. He is telling her how Mum forgot to buy enough batteries, but it was OK because Dad bought a battery charger. Amazing. Brilliant. Brilliant Dad.

Paula steps quietly to the hallway. She fetches out her ski-trousers as Kay clatters past her, back upstairs to Dad and the Gameboy. He does not stop to ask what she's doing. Paula puts on ski-trousers and jacket, gloves, cap with ear-flaps. She kneels down and reaches into the rack at the side of the cupboard, and takes out her skates. Just then Maudie stumbles through the door, her eyes glazed with sleep.

'Mom,' she pipes. 'Where're you going?'

'Ssh. Nowhere.'

'Why're you putting on all your stuff?'

'Maudie, go on back to the living room. D'you want another video?'

Paula keeps the videos hidden. The children are not allowed more than one each day. Maudie's face brightens, she nearly fastens on the bribe, then, 'Can I come with you? Please?'

'No, Maudie. It's too cold.'

'I've got my new snowsuit.' Maudie is already pulling off her slippers. 'Please Mom, please.'

'No,' says Paula, and she picks up her skates. She opens the door to a slice of freezing air and turns her back on Maudie.

'Go on back in the house. *Now*.'

The track rings under her boots. Frost seized the ground suddenly, weeks back, leaving steely ripples of mud. Over there, behind the fir trees, is the slim frozen tongue of the lake. It is shallow here, spread out into fingers on which the cottages sit. Paula walks fast to the shore.

She sits on a rock and fits on her skates. They have skated most days and the bay is full of blade-marks. But they have not gone far. And Kay had been stupid, throwing stones on to the ice. She slapped him for it –

'What if someone broke a leg because of you?'

Usually they take their broom down to the lake and sweep a small rink for themselves, but this year there is no need. There is no snow on the ice. Paula knows where it is safe to skate. She has been coming here all her life, and even if she hadn't she would be safe this year. There has never been a frost like it. The whole lake is solid, even by the springs. There are not many people here for Christmas this year, because there is no snow. Today the lake is bare. She looks south and sees where it widens, the ice pale and empty, waiting for her. She stands up, staggering a little on her skates, as the wine she drank at dinner sings in her head. It is so cold. Her face is covered but for a strip of flesh around her eyes. She is ready. She bends forward, puts her weight on her right blade, pushes off. The ice is perfect. In a few strokes she shoots out beyond the churned ice. She will do some figures first. She never has time when the kids are there, pestering her to watch them, to admire them. Eric doesn't like to skate, never has done. She does a T-stop, turns to shore, prepares to skate backwards and then come round in a tight circle, just there – And there's Maudie, running down the bank, her red cap flapping, her skates in her hand.

'Mom! Mom!' she screams, 'Wait for me!'

Paula stands frozen. There is Maudie in royal blue on the shore, waving frantically. There behind her is the sweep of fir which hides the cottage where Eric and Kay crouch over the Gameboy, and the spare set of batteries recharges in the battery charger Eric has been thoughtful enough to buy and bring all the way up here without telling Paula. Three hisses escape through the fine wool scarf which hides Paula's lips.

'Batteries. Jesus. Christmas.'

Something wicked gets into Paula. She turns away and sets her eyes on the glazed horizon where the lake's mouth spreads. She pretends she has not seen Maudie, has not heard her, has not understood that the child has followed her mother and is struggling with her skate-laces, too late and slow and clumsy to catch up. A mean wind cuts across the ice. It's too cold to stand still, Paula tells herself. Her weight tilts, her skate glides, she begins to move.

A cry tears out of Maudie and follows her. This time she doesn't call for her mother. It is just a scream. Maybe she took off her gloves, thinks Paula. Maybe the metal of the skate-blade has stuck to her fingers. She won't have fastened her cap. Her ears. She's got frost-bite. She slows, turns as if she's only been practising a circle, and skates back to Maudie.

Maudie is crying. Her mouth is open and she has not fastened her new red cap. Her fingers fumble as she sobs. She can't see to do up her skates. Paula looks at the smeared, teary face and frantic fingers and a wave of love and hate picks her up and throws her far, farther than it has ever thrown her before. She kneels down in front of Maudie and fixes her laces, then snaps the cap down over Maudie's ears. Maudie has taken off her gloves to do up the skates, just as Paula has always told her she must not. Maudie's fingers get mixed up and slide into the wrong spaces and Paula puts them on.

'Can I – can I come with you?' hiccups Maudie.

'Yes,' says Paula. She is not going back to the cottage with this child.

The two of them step out on to the ice. Maudie is a good skater, like her mother. In the city Paula takes her to classes at the rink. But Maudie shrinks closer to her mother at the sight of the huge white lake opening out in front of them.

'Come on,' says Paula, 'skate behind me and I'll keep the wind off you.' There is no wind but the wind of their passage. Paula skates fast, leaning into the space that offers itself to her. She hears the child behind her and knows Maudie is following, keeping up with her. The low grey sky is heavier than ever today. Surely it is going to snow.

They've never been so far out. Paula glances back and sees the five inlets, five fingers, disappearing into the woods where the cottages are. They are on the open lake where the ferry runs from shore to shore in summer.

'Mind the branch, Maudie!' she calls back, and Maudie swerves in her mother's blade-marks. The branch is frozen into the ice, sticking up a fist of wood. Paula skates faster. She is warm now, her legs moving easily, her arms tingling with life. She could skate like this for hours.

'Mother!' calls Maudie. Paula slows, turns, circles Maudie.

'What is it?'

'Mother, where are we?'

'Why, we're on the lake. Out on the lake where we take the boat.'

Maudie looks round, skating beside her mother now, glancing at the low black line of the shore and the huge nothing between her and home. 'I like it here,' she offers, looking up at her mother's face.

'Do you?' says Paula, but she looks out, way away from Maudie, smiling, and so she doesn't see the tip of Maudie's left skate catch on a rough place in the ice, and Maudie hang for a second at awkward half-stretch and then crash down on the ice. But she hears it. She is with Maudie in a second. Maudie is white, cawing from the bottom of her chest. Her breath has been knocked out of her. Paula gets her up, sits her, supports her while Maudie fights to breathe. She mustn't sit on the ice, thinks Paula, she will freeze. Maudie's nostrils spread wide, reaching for air. The first breath Maudie gets she uses to cry. Paula holds her, Maudie with her heavy little skates dangling, her red cap twisted sideways, her cheek beginning to ooze reddish, purple blood.

Its OK, baby,' says Paula, hoisting Maudie higher, 'show me where it hurts now.' But Maudie cries and scrubs her face against her mother, clinging to her with her legs so the sharp blades dig through Paula's ski-trousers.

'Come on, birdie,' says Paula, 'Show me your face. Come on bird-spice.' She hasn't called Maudie that for years. Why did she think of it? The snowsuit is so bulky she can scarcely feel Maudie through it. No broken bones, though. She is frightened, not hurt.

'Maudie,' she says, 'Maudie. You've got to be a big girl now. Look around.' Maudie puts her head out and peeps over the puffy horizon of Paula's snowsuit shoulder.

'We have to get back,' says Paula.

'Carry me,' says Maudie.

'I can't,' says Paula, 'Not that far.' She feels Maudie let her body go floppy in her mother's arms. She looks down. Maudie has shut her eyes tight, the way she does when she wants to be carried upstairs to bed. Eric always carries her in the end, after Maudie's begged and pleaded and pretended to be asleep.

'No,' says Paula quietly, 'this is real, Maudie. You have to skate.' Maudie doesn't understand, she knows. She is a city child, not like Paula, who grew up here and always knew that winter was hungry, just waiting for you to make a mistake. It got someone every year. Hunting accidents, frost-bite, a boy skating too late into the Spring. Maudie doesn't know about any of that. Why should she? They're summer and Christmas visitors with a car-full of things from the city.

But Maudie understands a certain tone in her mother's voice. She lets Paula put her down on the ice and brush off her snowsuit.

'Take my hand,' says Paula.

They skate slowly, side by side. Maudie is pale. She puts her head down against the bitter air which cuts into her face.

'I'll look out for both of us,' promises Paula. She scans the ice for branches, stones, rough places which might catch Maudie's skates. They have come a long way out, much farther than she thought. She sees something dark on the ice, swerves, stops.

'It's a bird,' says Maudie, 'What's the matter with it?'

The bird is dead, lying on its back, its claws hooked. It is perfect. Nothing has touched it.

'It must have just fallen,' says Paula, 'It wasn't here before. Look, this is the way we came, you can see our skate-marks.'

'Why did it die?' asks Maudie.

'I don't know. I expect it just froze. You know what Mrs Svendson said, about the birds in her yard?'

Maudie puts out her hand and touches the bird. It is already hard, its eyes open but shrouded. She picks it up and holds it flat on the palm of her glove. Wind ruffles back its feathers.

'It's a redwing,' says Paula. 'See,' and she shows Maudie the markings.

'It just fell out of the air,' says Maudie. She has forgotten her own fall.

'Yes, I think so.'

'How fast did it fall?'

'Not very fast. It isn't hurt.' Maudie looks up, as if to see a sky drifting with the slow fall of birds. She pats the redwing again.

'Can we bury it? Can we make it a little grave?'

'No Maudie. We can't skate all that way back carrying it.'

'But if we leave it here, an animal's going to eat it.'

'That's OK, Maudie. It'll just stay here in the quiet. That's what happens to birds when they die. And when it snows it'll cover up the bird like a blanket all winter.'

Maudie puts her face close to the bird's beak and frozen eyes. 'He wants to stay here,' she says finally, and she lays it down on the ice.

'Good girl,' says Paula. 'Now let's go.'

When they reach the shore Maudie is too stiff even to sit and have her skates taken off. Paula lifts her, skates and all, and lugs her up the slope through the trees to the cottage. The lights are on, marking the ground and making it dark where Paula and Maudie come up the track.

'I bet they're still playing with Kay's Gameboy,' says Maudie, 'He won't ever let me play.'

'Oh well,' says Paula, 'he only had it today.'

'Yeah,' says Maudie, 'anyway Kay didn't go out on the ice. None of us've ever been that far before, have we?'

'No.'

'You and me are the only ones who got to do it,' says Maudie, 'Next Christmas I won't fall over. We'll skate all the way. Right down the lake. Can we?'

'Yeah,' says Paula, 'If you still want to.'

They go in and shut the door. That night, in the dark, when Maudie and Paula are asleep, it starts to snow.

The Madonna of Mortimer Close

Mary Ciechanowska

When Kate, my younger daughter, ran through the latest list of what she'd like for Christmas, one November afternoon some years ago, I only half-heard her at first. I smiled and nodded, vaguely, I expect.

I'd just got in from my turn to do the home run, bring five children back from far-flung Clement Attlee Primary and deliver the three who weren't my own on some pretty scattered doorsteps. All on bus and foot; I still wasn't driving. I was sitting on the sofa with my mug of Nescafé, getting my strength back and thinking. About the part-time teaching job I'd recently gone back to, and what to take out of the freezer, and when to phone Aunt Beatrice in Yorkshire to ask her down to Putney over Christmas; my uncle had died since the last one and she hadn't any children to invite her. So I'd only been half-listening to Kate.

But then the words sank in. I was surprised.

'Are you sure, Kate?' I said. 'A baby doll?'

Neither Kate nor her sister Lucy had ever gone in much for dolls. Unless you counted the knitted Polish sailor from Stefan's Warsaw cousins that had seen Lucy through the tonsillectomy. And somebody had given them a talking doll once, it said 'Will you be my best friend?' in a stage-school lisp. They'd shoved it at the back of the shoe-cleaning cupboard. It's probably waiting there still.

The apples of Kate's eyes had always been her twenty-seven animals, chiefly a disgruntled-looking bear. Taking them all off the bed at night so that she could get in gave us useful regular exercise.

'Sure I'm sure,' she said (we had a family from Wisconsin in the Close at the time). 'A Sasha baby doll.'

You may remember Sasha dolls? Made in Scandinavia, and in all good toyshops then. They had this very progressive image, they were supposed to look more like real, live children than other, more dimpled makes. In my view they didn't, though, the Sasha designers had overstated they seemed a bit too sensible and pure, You couldn't imagine a Sasha laughing as it farted in the bathwater, for instance, or getting chocolate all over the chair arms. Sashas wouldn't even eat chocolate, they'd be much too dentally-aware.

They came in three varieties – the girl doll, the boy and the baby. You could see they were related, they all had exquisite arm-positions and distant, rather spiritual expressions. The baby, that Kate wanted, was the worst in this respect. *Its* gaze verged on the nirvanal.

'So you're sure you're sure?' I said.

'Jane's got one,' began Kate, ticking off. 'And Laura, and Rebecca, and Joanne, and Angela and Yoko. Even daft Harriet Hathaway. And Sarah says she's getting one for Christmas.'

I saw the pressures then. Jane had got hers first, apparently, to make up for having a new sibling, and then Laura had remembered that she had one at home, and the two of them had triggered off a boom. Clement Attlee Primary's Middle Infants was now lap-deep in soulful-looking babies with appealing arms. Mrs Hillaby had had to start a shelf for them, Kate said. They'd already been getting in her way a lot, and then the headmistress had had to tell Jane and Laura off in front of the whole school for arguing over their ones in Assembly, all the way through 'Sing Hosanna'. That was the last straw, Mrs H had muttered, gathering them on to her shelf. But she let the owners have them back at playtimes.

'What do they do with them then?' I asked.

'You don't *do* anything with them, Mum. You just *have* one. You walk around with it and all look at each other's. Jane lets me have goes with hers sometimes. Everybody's got one now. Except for me and Sarah and a few of those people on the door table.'

I went in search of ours that very week; I guessed that there might be a local shortage. Finally, I found one, in a toy shop the other side of Barnes that called itself Learning Through Play. It was the last of its kind until after Christmas, they said, there had been an incredible run. They knocked something off the price for me because the nose was slightly shop-soiled; I was sure that I could get it out with Ajax.

I bore the package home across the Common feeling favoured and successful, and pleased with myself as a parent. I swaddled it away on the top wardrobe shelf, where Stefan throws the vests I'm always shrinking.

It's all right, about your doll,' I said to Kate that night.

'Good! I can hardly wait! Harriet Hathaway's mother's knitting lots of things for hers. She's doing a purple baby-gro next.'

'Does Harriet's mother work?' I asked, kindly, but Kate didn't hear.

'I think I'll have it for St Nicholas' Day,' she was deciding. 'Then I won't have to wait for it so long.'

Stefan's being Polish made 6 December St Nicholas' Day, a special one in our house, rather like a trailer for the main event. It was better than the twenty-fifth in some ways. There wasn't all the cooking to do, for one thing (or if there was, in Poland, I'd Anglicised that bit out). And for another, although the whole point of St Nicholas' Day is children getting presents, the girls didn't have enough of them to bring on Christmas night-style blues. On St Nicholas' morning they woke, not all that long before the usual time, (the lack of small hours frenzy was another St Nicholas' plus) to sweets, a pound coin or two well buffed up with Brasso, and one good item each off the Christmas list.

Aunt Beatrice didn't want to come at first. She wasn't talking religion, she said, I knew her better than that, but there was still a lot of Jack in the air there for her, she didn't want to leave the place just yet. And on the other hand – she knew it sounded confusing, but that was how it was – she wanted to face up to the fact of Christmas without him, and she'd have to be at home to do it properly.

She said, 'The sooner I face up, Jill love, to how things really are, the sooner I'll feel better.'

Typical Aunt Bea, I thought, strong on the feelings, even stronger on the facing up. Do you remember in the *The Deer Hunter*, the Robert De Niro character who's sensitive at bottom but knows what life's about, pointing at his own finger and saying to this friend who's going through a reality crisis, 'Look, Jake (or Sam, whoever), *this is this*!'? It reminded me very much of my aunt. She's an extremely 'this is this' type of woman.

Kate was particularly fond of her. When she heard she wasn't coming she hunted out her latest postcard of the Living Steam Museum and wrote, 'Please come, Auntie Bea, there's some Uncle Jack in our air as well from when he helped Mum with the kitchen floor tiles and I'll be getting a Sasha for St Nicholas' Day so please come.'

Beatrice rang the next night. She'd pop down after all, she said, but only for a day or two, round about the sixth.

Everyone woke together on St Nicholas' morning; Lucy's one good item was an alarm clock that roused you to the sound of horses' hooves coming at you from one far horizon and disappearing, in time, over the other.

After that had run its course we could hear paper being rustled and then contented cries from Kate that we took to be the motherlove dawning. Then we heard the clock again, then more maternal murmurings. Then a silence that I knew wasn't right.

Both girls' voices, then, in some sort of urgent consultation. Finally, a furious cry: 'It's a boy!'

There were stomping sounds across the landing, and then Kate was standing over me. The brown bear glowered at me from the crook of one arm. From the other hand hung the now naked doll.

'It's a boy!' Kate gnashed. 'It's got a penis!'

I sat up in bed. 'Let's have a look.'

She dropped it on my duvet. She'd got it right, of course; conscientiously modelled yet faintly other-wordly, it reminded me, in style, of the face.

'I'm sorry,' I said. 'I didn't realise. That they made *these* in both sexes, too. The baby ones as well.'

It *was* quite unusual, in baby dolls, then. But that was no excuse. I should have checked, I knew the Sasha image.

'Does it matter, really, all that much?' I said. 'It's exactly like the girl one in every other way.'

'*Mum!*'

Kate's shriek galvanised Stefan. In the face of all the odds he had been trying to snuggle down again but now he sat up, rapidly. He sighed 'Happy St Nicholas', folks!' – He knew a long haul when he saw one, and he got his feet into his slippers and himself down the stairs in less time than it normally takes him, opening one eye. To make my aunt a cup of tea, he called back over his shoulder.

'Of *course* it matters!' Kate went on, hardly cutting down on the pitch. 'I don't want a *boy* one, do I?'

I have seldom heard a question sound quite so rhetorical.

At this point Aunt Beatrice came in, wearing Stefan's old dressing gown that she'd found on the hook on the spare room door. I glanced around, and thought how very Christmassy the room was getting – Kate in her nightie, my aunt's gaunt form in the brown and beige stripes, the little male figure in the trough of my duvet, the bear that might just have been an ox . . . All we needed was an ass, I thought, and I could be that, for not checking the gender in the shop. I wanted to laugh, fleetingly. One look at Kate warned me not to.

'What a lovely baby doll!' Aunt Beatrice exclaimed, feigning unawareness. It *had* to be the feigned sort, unless she'd gone stone deaf overnight. 'Is that your new Sasha doll, then, Kate?'

'No!' snapped Kate. 'It's not! I don't want it. It's got a penis. I don't want it. I want a girl one. It's a boy.'

She looked from Aunt Beatrice to me.

'No, Kate,' I said, forestallingly. 'Don't ask me to. I'm not taking it back. It was the last one they had so we can't just do a swap.'

Kate's mouth went down at the corners.

'And they reduced the price,' I said, 'Which always makes it trickier, getting the money back.'

Her lower lip started to jut. 'Apart from which,' I added,

coming to my main reason last, 'It just seems' – I groped for the exact word – 'wrong.'

Kate flopped down on the rug and began to cry.

'Why?' she moaned, between sobs. 'Why, Mum? Why? Why? Just tell them it's a *boy*! They'll understand.'

Lucy joined us, cradling her clock.

'Just tell them it's a boy, Mum,' she said, climbing in beside me. 'They'll understand.'

'The problem is . . .' I began, 'The whole point is . . .' I wasn't sure precisely where to start.

'Your mother's position *is*, love,' Aunt Beatrice took up, briskly, 'that she doesn't think she ought to let you take it back, just because it's the wro –, just because it's an *unexpected* sex. She thinks it would be bad for you. She thinks it would be giving you the wrong ideas about what matters in life and she wants to bring you up with the right ones. You ought to try to see things from your mother's point of view.'

'That's *it*!' I said, gratefully. 'It's just like Auntie Bea says. I think it would be giving you a mistaken view about . . . well, people. What they're worth. What really matters about them.'

Lucy fiddled with the winding key; Kate sobbed, 'I don't want a boy!'

'Their individuality coming first,' I said, 'and all that.'

'The others have all got girls,' Kate wept. '*Their* mothers got it right!'

The clock went off. We waited.

Then Lucy said, '*You* wanted girls, Mum. When you had *us*. You *told* us.'

'Yes,' I said, 'But that's just it. I wanted girls, but if you and Kate had happened to be boys I'd have loved you just the same. In no time at all I'd probably have been thinking I'd really wanted boys all along.'

I looked down at Kate. 'You wouldn't be able to reject it if it were a real baby, would you, just because it was a boy?'

The crying stopped. Kate seemed to be considering. Perhaps we were coming to a breakthrough, I thought. Perhaps I'd have time to eat some breakfast after all.

'It's not a real baby. It's a doll,' she said at last.

A thoughtful silence followed.

Then: 'It's not a real baby. It's a doll,' my aunt repeated. Slowly, in her most cogitating tone.

She turned to me. 'I think Kate's got a point, Jill love,' she said.

We all trooped to Barnes after school; Stefan wouldn't be back in time to drive us, and Liz at number six, who owed me a couple of favours, wasn't in. My aunt's feet worried me, it's a good bit further than a stroll. But she was fine, she said, with Jack's old sheep-working stick that she took everywhere with her now, Barnes and back had nothing on her nearest dale.

I'd kept the receipt, of course, but Learning Through Play weren't very keen to make the refund at first. The owner was a man, perhaps that was why, perhaps he was unconsciously affronted. Or maybe he, too, objected on grounds of principle, it was an *extremely* educational shop. Or it could have been he didn't want the nose-speck back – you could still see it, faintly, in spite of the Ajax, under his flourescent strip.

He was OK in the end, though – keying in his till, in fact, when Kate spotted this beautiful German-made giraffe that she fell in love with instantly. She said she wasn't so sure about the doll any more, she thought the mix-up might well have put her off. The craze would probably be over soon, in any case. So we took the giraffe and paid the difference.

Then we had a cup of tea along Barnes High Street. And then we plodded back to Putney, single file across the Common in the winter dusk. It was a cold night, and full of seasonal atmosphere – the crisp, dark space around us, more of the same above, my aunt's stick whispering our progress through the rimed grass. And Kate, crooning very softly to her new giraffe.

When we'd almost reached the Red Rover we thought we saw a shooting star ahead. But it wasn't, it was the tail-light of a plane striking out across the sky from Heathrow.

Greetings

Moy McCrory

It started when my mother was over last night. She was in a sulk because I'm holding back on the arrangements for Christmas. Every year since I got married we've been over to her. For once I'd like to stay at home. She said 'I expect you'd rather be with your hoity-toity-in-laws' and does this line about those who think their parents aren't good enough. 'You'd introduce me as the cleaner given half a chance.'

It's got nothing to do with that, and anyhow I'm not going to Rupert's mother's though God knows why I shouldn't. I tell her I want to spend Christmas at home with my family and she says 'That's all right then. What time do you want me and Dad to arrive?' My face must have dropped. Then she said 'I see. We're not wanted.'

I'd been writing cards all evening and sticking them down and what with doing that and her talking about her legs I got confused and couldn't remember whose I'd done.

She'd just said she'd drop the ones I'd finished in the post-box because her doctor told her it's good to walk varicose veins and of course she has to read all the envelopes.

'Who's this?' she says.

'No one you'd know.'

Then she starts. 'You're so secretive. You used to bring your friends home. What happened to that Pam?' and I say 'That was years ago, we were at school together.'

I kept on writing an envelope so I wouldn't have to look at her when she said 'You've already written them one. I'm sure I've seen it. Look I've got it here' and she waves it at me. So I open it and I've done the same as last year, when I lost my rhythm and had to steam open a dozen. So she starts ripping them out before I can stop her and they're all wrong.

'This is the culprit,' she says. Then she looks inside 'Who's Mrs Collins?' and I tried to take it from her but she's already read it like she used to when I was a kid and she'd have all my birthday cards opened before I was down the stairs. Then she gives me a hard look and says 'What's this?' because I've signed it 'Frieda'. 'What are you playing at Maureen?' So I laugh. 'Oh that's Frieda Collins,' I said. 'Look what I've done. Well spotted.' 'Who's Frieda Collins?' she says. 'An old girl who lives round here. On her own for Christmas. She'd think she's sent herself a card! So I wrote out another, signed it 'Maureen' and made sure I kept it by my elbow.

I hadn't stamps enough for all of them so I kept some back. Soon as she'd gone to exercise her varicose veins I tore that one up and stuck it down the waste disposal. Then I fished out the one signed 'Frieda'. It's too difficult to explain to her.

She wants to know everything, always has. 'Where did you meet her then?' she'll say looking at an envelope. 'At work.' 'I don't remember you knowing anyone called that?' 'Why the hell should you?' Then she says soft things like, 'How come you have so many cards? You don't know anybody.'

In a way I think she might be right. Now we've moved here I don't see anyone, except for her, more's the pity. She's determined, I'll say that for her. There's not many sixty-eight year olds would get themselves on and off three buses and still play pitch and putt at the weekends.

'How many cards did you send last year?' she asked me. She knows. 'Two hundred!' she says. I explain it's to do with his job, clients and what not, but then she goes in for the kill. 'But you never see anyone do you?'

That's why I send cards. I'll not see Mrs Collins. Not her real name either, but we keep up appearances.

It's all appearance. Let yourself go and you've only got yourself to blame. And you'd be surprised who notices. Sometimes when I'm walking I think I'm being watched. It's not unlikely. I don't mean by spies, international agents, more's the pity – I could do with the excitement, no, I just mean from sly windows in the road.

It's when I'm out there, walking to nowhere in particular that I become aware of all those anonymous eyes. Eyes which glance up, eyes which watch as I pass. So I smile at the top of my daughter's head where it sticks out over the pushchair, let them see I'm contented, a happy woman. Doesn't do to look too miserable.

I can't help it. It's in my genes. The corners of my mouth turn down, even when I'm smiling. I think looking happy must be a physical trick. 'Smile!' people tell me when they point the camera and I'm already smiling. I suppose it's just got further to come for some of us and I'm one of the unlucky ones.

But you'd be surprised what people read into you. They see you the once and their mind's made up. When I was on maternity leave, before we moved here for the garden, I was on a reading blitz of travel stories – it's because we never had a honeymoon – I used to devour four or five a week. And that woman came up to me, the one who wheels the trolley in the library.

'I saw you. Last week,' and her voice didn't half carry. 'I thought you didn't look well. You were waiting by the bus stop and I was sailing past. You were waiting down at King's Cross.' The way she said it, 'down at King's Cross,' like I was there for passing trade.

I remember, it had been a freezing Tuesday and I'd gone into town. Time on my hands. I thought it'd be great. Meet friends for lunch, do things other people do. But everyone I knew was at work. Couldn't get away, and I'm walking round feeling tired and heavy, thinking 'these are your last weeks of freedom' – only I was bored.

I must have looked washed out that day. I was huge anyroad. That's why I was getting a bus. Couldn't face the last leg up the hill. But she went on, 'I thought you didn't look well,' and she shook her head. Then, right out of nowhere 'Problems at home?' and the way she looked at me. I hardly knew her. 'Problems at home' – and it didn't sound like a question.

They all looked up from the tables, even the assistants stared and God knows, they're educated.

Supposing there had been. Problems. I'm not saying there were, but supposing, did she think I'd tell her?

If there's something I can't stand it's these people who see trouble for you when you don't even know you're in it. Will they be told otherwise? Will they hell. Because you don't go round grinning like a lunatic they've got you down for chronic depression. Thing is, the more you say there's nothing the matter, the more they're convinced.

I used to go out with this fella, we'd hardly be out the house and he'd snatch his hand away and say 'What's the matter with you?' I'd say 'Nothing. There's nothing the matter,' and he'd say 'Yes there is.' So I'd say 'Well what is it then?' and he'd say 'I don't know, you tell me.' Then he'd complain. 'You should be more aware of your moods.'

'What are you talking about, I'm not in a mood,' and he'd say 'Oh really?' in this sarcastic way. There was no arguing with him. 'If you're not in a mood what are you getting so worked up about then?'

He'd tell me I didn't look happy. That's a crime, have you noticed? I used to disagree until one day I thought, 'This is ridiculous.' We were in the shopping mall and he'd gone on and on until I was ready to cry. I was hissing through clenched teeth 'I'm happy, OK?' Then he says 'Well why aren't you smiling?' I think it's very American, all this 'be happy' stuff. I'm just no good at it.

Ever since that woman and the trolley, now when I'm out on my own, I make the effort. It's easy. Quick mental check. That's fifteen minutes I think, give a little grin, it won't hurt you. I do. And now I'm a mother, you can bet there's someone itching to be an active citizen with a list of numbers for social services. I try.

Then my mother goes and says 'But you don't know anyone. Who are all these cards for?'

Soon as she was out the door I was on the brandy and polo mints.

I suppose she means well. But they haven't a clue what it's like for me here all day on my own. He's never here. At weekends he's preoccupied with paperwork. And don't think I'm some idiot that cooks dinners and irons shirts. They're all drip dry and he picks up the shopping. And he cooks when I can't be bothered, which is more and more these days. He leaves things on the freezer so all I've got to do is follow the instructions. My mother thinks he's wonderful.

'Your bloody father,' she says. 'Your bloody father couldn't boil an egg. I have to do everything. He'd starve to death in front of a tin of stew rather than warm it himself.' Then she tells me how women today don't know their luck.

'And you,' she says 'You just went to sleep and when you woke up you had a daughter. Call that giving birth?'

I've tried telling her it was a caesarean, because at forty no one's taking any chances, but will she have it.

'In my day,' she says 'women were women. My God the agony.' You'd think she had me in a field. I have to remind her. 'You were in a hospital' and she says 'No I wasn't. I was in hell.' Then she gets angry with me and says 'What more can you want?' God knows.

I was ticking off the days on the calendar when she came back. 'Can I smell disinfectant?'

I'd been sloshing it round the sink after I'd rinsed the glass. 'It's the cat. It's been sick again.'

'I'd have that thing put down,' she says. 'All it does is throw up. The house was reeking last time.'

I stayed in the kitchen with the felt tip until it was time for her to go.

I like to put a red line through the week on Saturdays. Gives me a feeling of satisfaction. I'm on the countdown to Christmas. Twenty days to go. Nineteen. Nearly missed that. It'll be the little one's first proper Christmas. Last year she didn't know what day of the week it was, just lay there. She'll be able to open presents, run round. Well that's one thing.

We didn't plan her, not really, we were arguing that winter and had a reconciliation. We'd always been careful. I thought I wouldn't have children. I wanted to do more in the department, but I could see there were no chances of promotion. It was Margery I felt sorry for, she'd been fifteen years with that firm, I'd only been there for three. We threw caution to the wind and bingo, at my age.

I'd arranged to go back after two months so I could get maternity pay and he said he'd do overtime then we'd review it. It hardly seemed worth it at the scale they offered me. I was working all week just to pay for child care. In three months I'd gone through nine childminders so I handed in my notice.

The boss was delighted, called me into his office for a sherry. 'A woman's place,' he told me. I'd have kicked him in the balls only I'd new patent leather slingbacks on and didn't want to get them scuffed.

I told him I didn't think all this 'woman's place' stuff had any relevance for today. It was economics, nothing else. Then he said 'Well, anyone could see you were missing the baby. You never looked happy.'

Actually, I fancied having time on my hands. Now, I'm not sure of anything. I feel unnatural sometimes because I'm not grinning my head off.

I do love her. She's beautiful when she's asleep. After she was born I couldn't bear to put her down. I wanted to cuddle her all the time. My mother was surprised. Told all the neighbours I was made-up with the baby. She couldn't believe the change in me. 'I never had you down as the maternal kind.' That's because she wasn't.

I suppose I must have looked happy then. Didn't stop to think about it. Anyone could see how pleased I felt. I still am. It's just, every day's the same. I dress us up nicely because I'm determined not to let myself go. Then I push her to the park in the afternoon. Well, it's good to have a routine. I get up with him. Drink a cup of coffee. He dashes out. I hear the car. I'm on my own till seven o'clock, some nights till nine depending on the traffic. You have to have a routine.

I used to like being on my own. You can sing, talk out loud, who's to know? As long as you're in control, I always say. I don't want to end up like Gran, she shouts at the TV. I talk away all day to the little one. She'll be making words soon, already she's pointing and making noises. She says 'moo' for mummy. But I miss conversation. I mean I've got the extremes haven't I? What with the baby and my mother – neither can talk sense.

I can't remember when he last sat down with me, don't know what we'd talk about. Can hardly ask him if he's seen anything interesting on telly, latest episode of *Neighbours*.

Actually, I saw this programme about women who discovered their husbands' 'infidelities'. Well it was more than that – some had second families, double lives, that kind of thing. Strangest was this woman who'd got an enormous valentine from her husband the day before he walked out on her.

She was cradling it like it was a baby. It was pink with this padded silk heart, not to my taste at all, but she thought it was wonderful.

She showed the cameras what he'd written. I thought that was wrong. Some things are between the two of you. She's reading out how she's the only one for him until the seas run dry, dreadful stuff, and then she says he just went to work the next day and never came back. And she read out this postcard he'd sent: 'I just can't go on any longer living this lie honey.' They both listened to country and western, so what can you expect?

When he came in I said, 'You could have all sorts of other women you know, because you're never here. You could have a family in Northumberland,' don't know what made me say Northumberland, it just came into my head, and he laughed. But you know, a couple of years ago, the thought wouldn't have crossed my mind.

We have less and less to do with each other. Maybe I ought to send him a Christmas card. We can go a week without saying more than a couple of sentences. At weekends he likes to flop round the house. I suggest picnics, outings. He wants to watch football. And now we don't even do the family shop together, that last great social custom – late night Friday at Sainsbury's.

We went once and had coffee in the cafe and the baby sat in a high chair. I was really proud because I thought we must have looked like a family, but he just wanted to get it over with.

I wanted the little one to ride the dolphin outside because I could have got in and held her and it would have been something to tell – 'How I Felt a Fool Riding Flipper', but no, he can't wait, 'There are other people wanting to get into our parking space.' He was the same in the café. 'There are other people wanting to use our table', so you scald yourself because you can't keep other people waiting.

'I need to go to the gents,' he says, 'Well don't be too long, there are other people wanting to pee.' Of course he thinks I mean myself. 'Here,' he says. 'You go first, I'll hold her.'

He's not inconsiderate. It was his idea to buy the washing machine. We'd always struggled to the launderette together on Wednesday evening. Took it in shifts. 'We can't go on like this,' he said, 'not after the baby comes.'

I used to walk past on the way back from the clinic. Sometimes I'd see Dora cleaning the machines. I'd nip inside for five minutes. But out here, well there's no launderette for miles. So it's a good job really.

I vary the route, walk down different streets. I haven't a clue where people go during the day. I walk round on my own. And the local library's not easy, two buses, and then a walk. There's a mobile that comes round. It's a sort of bus and if you can't order from the computer you're stuck with what's on the shelves. I've never seen anything like it. Romances, historical sagas where every second line someone's saying 'These are troubled times Victoria'. I've practically stopped reading. My mother told me she'd have to give up too but that was because she had the wrong prescription. Now that's sorted out she's quite happy in the large print section.

I was just walking back from the mobile, must have been October because the weather was turning cold. It had been such a mild autumn. I was pushing my daughter ahead of me when I turned down this road and I thought, why not knock on a door for a laugh? See if anyone comes? I can always act soft, pretend I've got the wrong house if anyone's in, like we used to when we were kids. That's another thing. You never see kids out playing do you? Anyroad, I think, why not? Might find out what's behind the curtains.

I think I look all right. I'm not frightening and besides I've got the child. I'd hardly be a burglar with a push-chair. So I went up to the one with the tidiest garden. If they can keep their herbaceous borders neat they must be decent people. I rang the bell. My heart was pounding. If anyone had come I would have died on the spot.

There was no sound inside so I stood there and I was feeling quite shaky, because it's not like me to be so daring, going up to a strange house, and I turned to walk back down the path.

I wasn't really disappointed. No one lives in those houses. I've always known it. They harbour ghosts. So, I'm just walking away when I hear something and someone's looking at me because when I glance back the net curtain sort of jumps.

I kept thinking about it. Over and over. Didn't mention it to him. He said I was preoccupied. Started talking about the problems he'd had at work, and usually I'm kept in the dark.

Funny that; the more you're interested they less they want to give. Like courtship. Not that he's romantic. When he finally asked me all he said was 'Oughtn't we to get married?' and I said something noncommittal like 'Suit yourself'. I blame my mother. She used to say, 'Play hard to get.' Look where it got her.

I suppose it was different then. Women didn't expect much. Now she comes round here, goes through all the rooms. I keep them neat. Nearly kill myself after she rings up.

'I'm coming over tomorrow.' She plans it like a military campaign. 'I'll be on the one-thirty from the roundabout,' and I'm out in the kitchen washing the floor. He says 'She doesn't come over to inspect the house. She comes to see her granddaughter.'

I tell him, he doesn't have to sit here watching her eyes flitter round the kitchen.

'Haven't you done the breakfast things?' she says, and then she's running her finger over the wall units.

'You need to get that skirting done.' That's what she greeted me with last time. I brazen her out – 'Do I?'

'Oh the women today, they aren't a patch on what they were.' Thank God for gun laws that's what I say or I'd have been in court years ago.

Whenever she phones up, I've got nothing to say to her. I always know its her. No one else rings during the day. I leave it. Then in the evening he'll pick it up and she'll want to know where I've been. 'Your mother said she phoned eight times this morning.' Don't I know it.

Well a few days after I'd rung the doorbell, I was going to the park, smiling into the air, just in case, when I found myself on the same road again. Don't know what possessed me, I'd popped in the newsagent's and bought some envelopes and left a box of matches on the counter. So I went back. I was passing the house and I thought if they'd seen me the day before, they might expect me to try again? Makes sense.

So I went up the path talking all the while to the little one so they can see I'm not a maniac or an encyclopaedia salesman. Then I can say 'I am sorry, I've got the wrong street' and they'll know I'm not some busybody if they ever spot me again.

Before I'm halfway up the path I know they've seen me. There's the same plucking at the curtain. I ring the bell. Stand there with a big grin on my face. I've taken the precaution of addressing an envelope to myself like it's a letter from someone that I'm trying to match up.

I can hear this shuffling. Then there's the sound of something slapping shut and in the back I see a metal bin lid rolling. I nearly jump, but it's a cat, a heavy old Persian with white tips on his ears, and he comes over to me. The little one squeals with delight and reaches towards it so we're both bent over this cat when I hear the front door opening behind me. The hairs on the back of my neck stand on end.

She's just standing in the doorway and doesn't say anything. She's got one of these security chains and it's across her face like a moustache. She's only about four and a half feet tall.

So I smile very brightly and ask for Martha. Now don't ask me how I came up with that, like Northumberland, it just came into my head. Only she's a bit deaf so I have to shout and I tell her I'm looking for Martha, only I think I've got the wrong address, and I spin out how I've just moved into the district, which is true and how I was at college with someone of that name, well it's half true. I was at college, not that I finished, but there again. I tell her how Martha and I were great friends – and then she's drawing the bolt off the chain.

'My daughter hasn't lived at home for nearly thirty years.' Either she hasn't heard me properly or she's got a daughter called Martha, and I'm trying to work out by the laws of coincidence the rate for this happening when she asks me which college it was, so I know I can excuse myself saying it must have been a different Martha only she nods and says, 'Yes that was it. But she'd be older than you. Are you sure?' I can't think of anything to say. Then she asks me how old the baby is and she's invited me in.

All the time I'm thinking how I can 'discover' that it's not the same Martha because I feel awful, when she goes and gets this photo album. Well I won't be in any of the photos so I'm all ready to profess stupidity and she says, 'Of course she changed her name.' So I stab out Collins, and this old one just nods, 'Yes, that was before she married. She became Jones.'

Well she was having me on. There's no Martha, and she's no Mrs Collins, only by now she's got me calling her that, and I'm feeling angry because she's got photographs out and is pretending the woman is this Martha who I've invented, and I can see she'll agree to anything I say. So we have this daft conversation, where I'm making things up.

I say 'Did she keep up with the ice skating?' and this one nods and tells me 'Yes, she did quite well,' and I say 'That's funny after that terrible accident,' and she shakes her head, and says 'That was awful wasn't it?' So I say 'You don't hear of many one legged ice-skaters,' and she agrees and says she was an unusual girl.

'I heard she emigrated to America,' I tell her and she says 'Yes, but she came back after six years.'

'Did she marry that boy she used to go out with?'

'No,' she says,' She married a somebody Jones, but they got divorced.'

'Not Daffyd Jones,' I say, 'the tenor in the choir?' and she says

'No,' she doesn't think so, 'It was someone she met in America, an American. Long ago.'

And then she asks me how I could have been in her daughter's year, because her daughter was so much older than me – 'She was born during the war.' So I say I was very advanced, thinking I'm going to give the game away any minute.

'Any children?' I ask and she says no.

'Shame that. Well I'd like to get in touch with her?' I mean I've got to say something, and the old one says, 'But she's dead.' Just like that. Kills her in a sentence.

Those photos probably were of her daughter. The old woman's got rings on. She can't be Collins though. Then she asks me my name, because I never told her. I call myself Frieda, a character in a novel I'm reading.

'Yes,' she says. 'She often spoke of you.' Then she makes me more tea and the baby's getting restless. Then she puts out these biscuits. Must have had them in the cupboard for months.

'I don't have many visitors,' she says.

Christ I'm not surprised. I was trapped there all afternoon and she starts talking about the War. She was widowed. Just the one child. Well she'd have to be older than me, but I leave it, and she's still pretending the girl was called Martha, just so I'll stay.

I call that sad. Both of us with this fake story. Then she starts weeping. The girl in the photos died.

I want to come straight with her, but it's too late. Then she starts calling the girl Evie. Recovers and says that was a family name.

'We always called her that at home. I bet she didn't tell you.'

'No,' I say.

'Poor Evie,' she says.

A car accident. Terrible really.

'Well I must go now.' And she's crying. 'Come again,' she says, 'I seldom go out, you'll find me at home most days.' Then there's a clatter and the old Persian comes in and sits on this armchair that's all covered in fur. 'Hello, Henry dearest,' she calls hin, so the little one's running after Henry Dearest and that takes another half hour.

The light is quite different when I get out. The sky is darker. I want to run; instead, I take my time. It might rain. I turn back to wave and she's not there, the door shut so quietly I didn't hear it.

She's a fraud. Never asked about the letter. I might have been genuine.

I don't walk down that road anymore, I always go the long way round. I know she sits there day after day. Waiting. Dreadful, these old folk with nothing better to do but lie to strangers, anything for a bit of company.

It's a rotten time of the year to be alone. I suppose we will have to go over to Mum's after all. She's taken up some damned night class and he's moaning because she leaves his tea in the oven. Then she tells me I'm lucky. Don't I know it.

It's just I can't bear all the arrangements. Every Christmas it's the same. Who are we going to have Christmas dinner with, his or mine? That's the way she puts it. Then she sulks when I don't immediately say 'You'. I want to stay here, but that would be worse. At least when you're visiting you can always go home. I can't feel excited. Not even the prospect of my daughter's face on Christmas morning. Must be something the matter. I should take some iron pills.

Soon be another whole year. Change the calendar. That's one thing. Lately I've started dreaming. That old woman, I see her face, and her nameless dead daughter. I see the pair of them watching me behind the curtains. I can't tell him about it. My mother says she's concerned then shouts at me to snap out of it. I asked her, 'Out of what?'

Last night she said I ought to be grateful. I've got a house, a child, a husband who's in work, and that's something these days isn't it?

My mother says women today are only out for themselves. I think she might be right. I don't know what else to be out for. Like I said, I don't think happiness is all it's cracked up to be.

Underneath the Almond Tree

Petronella Breinburg

It was not yet half-past-five, yet the Jamaican heat had made itself felt. And it wasn't even October when it was supposed to be the hottest. It's only December, thought Beverly. She resisted the temptation to hum a tune, not wanting to show the happiness she had felt over these last few days. Beverly was not the kind of woman who wanted her feelings known. That would have been a sign of weakness.

Although she had been warned that having cold baths was not the way to keep cool, she couldn't resist taking a shower. 'You get bad cold,' scolded the chambermaid, who was soon to become a friend.

After her almost-cold shower Beverly went out on to the balcony, to admire the mountains of Ocho Rios she told herself, but it was also partly to see if *he* was there strolling. 'Why should I be interested in his strolls?' she mused, smiling. I'm sure he doesn't admit that it isn't entirely coincidental that his early morning walks take him right past my veranda! He had once said that by five a.m. his room became too hot for his pale skin. But he was not there this time. Beverly half-closed her eyes, playing a childhood game. If you close your eyes tightly and concentrate hard enough, you can see anything you want to see, hear anything you want to hear, smell anything you want to smell.

She heard noises and running feet, heard the rustling of dry leaves, smelt the sweaty bodies of her ancestors running to free themselves from the horrors of Jamaican slavery. They ran behind those beautiful mountains which offered their shelter for people attempting to break the chains around their ankles, around their minds, around their thinking. Behind those mountains, Beverly thought, there is still dry blood, red blood dripped from feet cut off to prevent further running. Yet even without feet they had kept running, running, desperately short of breath, but still running. She heard the drums, and read their message. The drums were talking, warning, warning of captures, warning of danger, 'Danger, Danger!' the drums' beat shouted, 'Keep control, control,' the lighter Apinti drum was saying, 'Keep control!'

'Oh, morning mam you got up?'

'Merle, didn't hear you come in.'

'Me did knock but you no hear. You must not let your door unlock, it dangerous, dem think you got money!'

Beverly laughed and wondered if in her days in the Caribbean she would have felt pity for this poor woman, slaving from early in the morning to late at night, cleaning other peoples' houses for a pittance.

'Eh, we people don't come here, it too expensive for them, so dem think yu must be American.'

'I am not American and you're not Jamaican.'

'How you know dat?' the young woman began to remake the bed Beverly had already made up, as Beverly got ready to go down for an early coffee.

'Your accent and the way you speak; that is Guyanese fo' sure.'

'Oh look! De young man!' The young woman grinned 'he walk pass here twice already this morning. I saw him but he done know I saw him.'

'We work in the same office in London.' Beverly left the room and made her way to the lift which would take her five floors down to where early morning coffee was laid on for the guests of this 'luxury hotel', as it was billed in the new brochure. Yeah, luxury, she thought angrily, but for whose benefit? The Americans who controlled the local slaves. She swore mentally, 'Bastards! Paying the people pennies and charging the earth! Thank God the firm, and not me paying.' She arrived at the coffee table and found that *he* was already there.

'Hello. Milk?' He poured her some coffee.

'Thanks,' she said, and she could feel him turning away from her. He dared not look at her. She was fully aware that he felt uncomfortable in her presence and what's more she knew the reason why. It was a good sign. 'The lizard likes it when the fly is uncomfortable and nervous.'

She smiled inwardly, 'Milk, no sugar.' Lizard! she thought. You know I don't take sugar, you made me coffee often enough in the office.

Coffee in hand they strolled across to the rows of almond trees. He picked up an almond from the ground. 'Wonder if these are poisonous.'

'Liar, he knows it's almond, he's playing games with me, or he wants me to explain. I have Caribbean roots and so naturally I'm an expert on anything to do with the Caribbean!' She decided to go with the game: 'That's where the almond essence your mother uses for her cakes comes from.' She deliberately said mother instead of wife. She knew that he had no wife, talk of his divorce was all over the office grapevine, with many of the women battling for the position of second wife. There had been a great deal of relief when it became known that it was to be Beverly, fifteen years his senior, who would be going to Jamaica with him. Bev, so safe, a man-hater some said; Bev, project director, yet big sister to every one; Bev and him, chosen to represent the firm in the spectacular opening of The Tamarind Beach – hotel and leading business conference centre of Jamaica. It was Bev who would be spending a whole week there alone with him, but that was no cause for alarm. Even the 'Old Terror' thought Bev was safe – that's why he sent her instead of a younger woman.

Beverly noticed that some of the children at the resort were already up, well before their parents, who were probably too worn out after the late-night suggestive dancing which The Tamarind Beach put on every evening. The Tamarind, having made in all likelihood, thousands of pounds, had extended to cover the whole beach of Ocho Rios, including its own pier for the shiploads of tourists it expected once the extensions had opened on New Year's Day with a fanfare of activities – dancing, Jonkonnu, masquerade.

'You're miles away.'

She smiled at him but without actually looking away from the children, who were running around by the swimming pool, trying not to be caught by the young children's entertainer dressed as the Jonkonnu bogy man. Each time a child was caught they would be thrown into the pool, as the others counted: 'One, two, three . . . in!'

'You're thinking of your childhood?' It was a question and a statement all in one.

'We didn't have swimming pools, we had almond trees though.'

'Yes, you seem fascinated by the almond trees. Did something happen to do with an almond tree?'

'I wonder why holiday brochures in the Caribbean only show palm trees, never almond trees?' Bev said. She was not going to tell him about the almond tree of her childhood when she was as tiny as those children now swimming; the almond tree which had earned her, over some thirty years, the names – first of man-hater, then as big sister, good chaperone, protector of virgins! She got up and he followed. She strolled along the white sand and he went too, almost meekly. She strolled in silence and so did he. Eventually, she spoke. 'This sand is pretty, it looks like salt!'

'Now, it was she who was uncomfortable in his company. The waves lashing against the sea shore mocked her . . . She began to talk casually as if they were back at work in London, chatting about all the money the firm was or was not making from the technological age.

'I wonder how everybody else is getting on with both of us away?'

'You worry too much about them, let them carry on for a week without us slaves, eh?' Then he started with embarrassment at his use of the term 'slave'.

'Yah, a black slave and a white slave.' She succeeded in putting him at ease.

'Careful! White slavery means something different.' This time he blushed.

'Ah, breakfast! I can smell the freshly ground, Blue Mountain coffee . . . must get some to take home.'

'By the way, you're coming to the carnival thing tonight, aren't you? I know you don't take to these things, but this is The Tamarind's big night before the opening so I thought, maybe . . .' He tried to sound casual as if they were back at work discussing business, but failed.

'As long as I don't have to dance and rub my stomach against anyone.'

'No one would expect you to.'

'Oh, yeah?' Ever heard of a black woman who doesn't dance?'

'Dance and carnival jump-up are two different things.'

'Anyway, it's not a carnival, it's Jonkonnu!'

That evening, when she arrived on the beach where the dancing and floor shows were taking place, the music had already started. She had deliberately taken her time so that they did not arrive together. At the entrance she had to give her room number and name, then answer a very stupid quiz. When she gave the correct answer she was told that she had won a hat with a golden rim.

'Good publicity gimmick,' she laughed.

'You room five one seven?' asked a girl who was dressed, Beverly registered, as an old plantation woman with large artificial buttocks.

'Yes,' Beverly replied.

'Your friends are at table twenty-two, right up the front.' The huge artificial bottom strode off leaving Beverly to follow. By the table was the exact same group which had been working together that whole day, all talking about computers and technology.

'There you are! We were just talking about computerised music, but of course these people here know nothing about that,' one of them said.

Bloody hell, she thought, not more blinking business.

'Do sit down,' said one of the men.

Beverly stared at the roast pig on her plate. She had just seen the poor thing being rotated on a spit above an open fire.

Soon came the main event. A group of young dancers in Jonkonnu costumes and masks, had the crowd spellbound.

'What does this all mean, this Jonkonnu?' He was sitting opposite her.

'Some hocus-pocus going back to slavery, I am told,' said an older businessman.

'Yes, Jamaica was one of our leading slave colonies, now we're upset when they come to Britain,' responded another.

Then it was audience participation time and everyone joined in. Beverly was content to take photographs of the colourful event though mentally she kept *him* very much in sight. She saw him being dragged by the hand by a dancer and becoming part of the crowd jumping up to the rhythm of the steel band. Watching his misery – he certainly was no dancer – she wondered how long to wait before she rescued him.

After a short while she rose, took the hat she had won, and plonked it on her head. She waited until their eyes met. As soon as they did, he came towards her, much to the obvious disappointment of one of the young beauties planted there to extract as much money as possible from the guests.

'Ready to go?' he asked in that tender voice which worried her at times. It was that voice which made him deadly to many weak women. Luckily, I am not weak, she thought boastfully. 'I am, yes,' she answered.

They were both suddenly very silent as they made their way along the sandy beach, through the row of almond trees, to the towering block of luxurious rooms and suites waiting for their new beginning. Behind them the music was still blaring. They got to her room and they both knew what their choices were. He could stay or go back to his room. He decided to leave and she knew that he'd be in his room. She didn't need to phone to check on him.

The heat of the next morning woke her up. At first she thought that she must have overslept but when she checked the time she realised that it was not even five in the morning.

'God,' she groaned as she got out of bed. 'How can people live in this heat?' She had to have a cold bath, she didn't care if she caught a bad cold or not. After that, she stepped into the holiday short and shirt suit she had bought from the hotel shop, and then out on to the balcony as usual. She wondered where he was and what he was doing. Then she spotted him in the pool near her block. At first she did not recognise that nearly naked, pink body. But he must have noticed her for he began performing; doing tricks in the water, funny back strokes, back flips or whatever those swimming strokes were called. Like a performing seal, you are, she thought. I expect you want me to applaud or cheer. At least Romeo sang to his Juliet. At least back home even though she had spent most of her adult life in Britain, she still thought of her place of birth in the Caribbean as 'back home', young men sent serenaders to sing by the door of their loved ones. Even at a distance, the pink body in the water looked very attractive. But, he didn't have to be a performing seal to get her attention. After all, she'd been aware of him for a year now – ever since he first joined the firm.

She decided to go inside – as long as he knew that she was sitting there and watching he would stay in the water doing tricks. Poor darling is that all you can do to attract the attention of a lady? Or am I such an ogre that you have to risk drowning, doing those silly water dances!

There was a lot of chatter at breakfast. It was the last day for many of the special guests. That night would be the last night, not only of the year, but also of the old name of the hotel. There was to be an all night jump-up, bonfire and sea cruise heralding the New Year and the new Tamarind Renaissance Resort. Many guests were planning to 'hit the town' as they called it. Beverly and *he* went along but soon got left behind by others. There were people offering everything from expensive souvenirs, to beads made from coffee beans.

'Buy one mister, one for the lady.' The young woman came up to him holding out her hand, full of strings of beads. 'Blast!' Bev swore under her breath, 'they mob you!' But she bought three strings of beads. 'Three for good luck,' she said, as she placed the strings, one at a time around his neck.

The young woman cheered her approval: 'Good fi you lady!'

They went to the town centre, bought bags full of presents to take back and had lunch at a Chinese eating house.

'It's strange finding Chinese restaurants in Jamaica,' he said 'I'd like some Jamaican cuisine!'

The restaurateur came over, 'But I am Jamaican and this is Jamaican Chinese cuisine!' he laughed, and went into a lengthy history of Jamaica and all the various races who were thrown together by the British colonialists.

After the meal they took a bus to the famous Dunns River Falls.

At first she didn't dare get into the water. 'I can't swim,' she protested.

'You don't have to mum,' the guide encouraged. 'Everybody hold hands and you walk up and down the falls. It's fun.'

In the end she let him persuade her to hold his hand, and the guide's, then, barefoot, they went in, together with a crowd of people. It was beautiful. The water cascaded down on people, and they screeched with delight, some fighting to reach the top and winning prizes for doing so. But Beverly wasn't so ambitious. The water was cold and soon she had had enough of wading through it, trying not to fall over on those slippery rocks. She went off to a makeshift changing room where he helped her to dry her hair. From the look in his eyes she feared that he might cause a commotion by openly kissing her. He didn't. The look in her eyes must have warned him off.

When they got back to The Tamarind she was very tired and slept right through supper. A knock at her door did not wake her so he went to his room and phoned.

'You all right?' he asked, concern in his voice.

'Oh, yes, but what time . . . Oh my God, look at the time.'

'You've missed a lovely dinner. I knocked at your door but couldn't wake you. Anyway, I can order something up for you.'

'Mh, why don't you go and choose something and bring it up for me?'

'What do you want?'

'Whatever you would want for yourself. Something light, I suppose.'

'Right, done! Coming up, dinner for m'lady.'

'You're cheerful.'

'Well, it's the last day.' He paused briefly, 'The last of the old and the beginning of the new.'

She made no reply, but her thoughts wandered.

'Anyway, see you in a bit,' he said.

Soon, he returned, banging at the door. When she opened it, he rushed in with a tray, ladened down with food. 'There is a real Jonkonnu, down town, it's coming this way,' he said.

He placed the tray on the table then rushed out on to the balcony.

'I can hear them in the distance, let's go?' There was pleading in his eyes and she thought how green they were.

She hesitated. 'Not my kind of thing, too noisy!'

'Please. But – of course – no one can make you do anything you don't want to do.'

'Am I that much of an ogre?'

'You scare the pants off some people we both know.'

'And you, do I scare the pants off you?'

'You did at first, sometimes even now!' He blushed crimson.

She was standing very close to him, secretly enjoying his nervousness. She was laughing inwardly but made sure not to show it. Being so close to his face, she realised that he was not as young as he looked from a distance. 'Mh, about thirty-eight I'd say. The same gaps between Prince Charles and Lady Diana.' He read her thoughts and said, 'And you're not as old as you want us to believe . . . that's it . . . a safety net!'

She changed the subject quickly.

'Oh, there they are, I can see the crowd from here! 'Let's go!' As he turned she noticed that he was wearing the string of beads she had bought him.

In the street the crowd was huge, people were dancing, and the smell of perspiration was almost overpowering. She wondered why she had hated these things; jumping and dancing in the street, the smell of sweat hitting the air. Why was she so different to what people expected of her? Why wasn't she just a secretary – that's what black women with her schooling were supposed to be. Why wasn't it the other way around, he the boss and she the underdog, the one to be pitied? Why didn't she fall for those old boys, especially 'Old Dragon' with his twisted moustache? She laughed heartily. He could have misunderstood her laughter for he said, 'Hold hands,' and took her palm. 'So we don't get separated.' He had to shout above the noise. People were shaking their hips, rubbing their tummies against their partners, suggestively.

'This is like a mini carnival, only they've got masks. Some of them are frightening. What do they represent?'

'Don't know, we got to ask at the hotel.'

They were being pushed along with the crowd, and found themselves in a side street, 'Where are we?'

'No idea,' she replied and realised how tightly he was holding her hand. It was sending the blood rushing to her head. They came by the market square and she recognised that they had gone a full circle round the town centre.

'Oh, my feet,' she lied not wanting him to know that she had had enough of crowds and noisy music.

'Let's get back. Let's take the shortcut through the almond lane, unless you're scared of . . . what do they call it again, the thing that runs wild on New Year's Eve?'

'Dupy, spirits of our ancestors.'

He moaned, 'Spirit of Bev's ancesters, I come to wish you a new beginning.' He came up close and pretended to be strangling her.

'Stop! You're like a little boy.'

'Is that how you see me? As a little boy?'

She made no reply, resisting the temptation to pass her hand up and down his side.

Back at her delux room she flung the door open – 'Don't know about you, but I smell! It's all that sweat mingling with that stuff some of them smoke.' She made for the shower.

'What about your supper?' he called.

'What?' she shouted back, already under the water, which she made very warm this time.

'The patties, they're stone cold!'

'Don't want them!' She let the hot water run down her back her blood tingling, her legs deepening to the pink of lobsters' talons.

'How's the water?' he shouted from the table where he was sitting.

'God!' she thought, raising her eyes to the ceiling as if to ask some god for patience. She resisted the temptation to shout, 'Come and try it,' and instead shouted back: 'Hot and nice.'

Still damp, she came out of the shower, wearing a dressing gown, her hair wrapped in a beach towel.

'You'll catch your death . . .' He moved towards her and helped to dry her hair.

'Your hair didn't get different, not like Jasmine, remember that time?'

'Yes, that time at the outing, when we got soaked and her hair turned back.'

'Why?' he was standing behind her, successfully avoiding looking up to the mirror where she would have been able to see his face. She did not have to see his face in any mirror, she had a clear image of it in her mind. And she could feel his hand shaking, his breathing loud.

'That's because she uses straightening chemicals. I don't, this is my natural hair and my natural colour. I don't use skin lighteners either.'

'No, you're not the type. You're natural, that's what I like about you. But we used to be, well, I used to be scared of you. None of us dared step out of line.'

She smiled vaguely. 'Blast that music, they're not going to go on?'

'Oh, I like the drums, the rhythms get you. When I was a boy in Kenya . . .'

Christ, is he going to talk all night?

'Yes, I heard you lived in Africa?'

'I was born there.'

'So you're an African.'

'A white African.' He finished drying her hair. 'Well I had better go and leave you in peace.'

Jesus Christ, give me faith!

'Watch out the Old Year Jumby don't get you!'

'Yeah, what's this about a ghost at midnight, tonight?'

'Well, go and have your shower while I tell you about the ghost coming to put to rest the year 1992. Of course, in Guyana we call them jumbies, in Jamaica they're called dupies.'

In Haiti they have zombies,' he supplied.

'Wrong, a zomby is a living death, a jumby, or a dupy is the spirit of a dead person who is going to come tonight and see us into the New Year.'

'You trying to scare me, or what?' he shouted from the bath.

'No!'

Scare you? You're not as innocent as you make out mate, not after you had years of married life. Aloud she said, 'I'll tell you more jumby stories while you shower. I've got something clean that you can put on.' He looked strange in one of her sarongs: skinny legs and arms sticking out and his hair hanging down like Jesus Christ minus the beard – perhaps Jesus when he was a young man, a suntanned Jesus.

'Why are you laughing?' he asked, but she ignored him and continued to tell folk stories, both of them laughing until they felt intoxicated on their drinks of ginger beer. He had moved to lie down on the bed. Meanwhile, outside, the drums with their hypnotic beats echoing an African past, drowned out the westernised music.

'At school they made fun of me,' he murmured. 'I was skinny and I didn't like fighting or any of the 'rough neck stuff' and I mixed too much, so it was said, with what they called 'the blackies' and servants. And I have still,' he was almost whispering now, 'got problems.'

'What sort, HIV?' she asked casually.

'God no! Nothing like that! It's just that, er, I let people down. That was, I suppose, the trouble with my marriage.'

She understood at once. 'No chance,' she said. 'No chance. I am too experienced to allow you to let me down.'

She could tell that he was terribly scared. He looked paler than usual. His eyes looking up at her from the pillows had gone a deeper green.

'Well . . . I mean . . .?

If he don't shut up, I'll kill him! She placed her hand under his head, lifted it and gently placed another pillow under it. He was still shivering, yet he could not possibly be cold. Skillfully she took him along, past the almond trees on to the seashore, where the waves were awaiting. She felt him holding on to her as if his very life depended on her, tighter and tighter he gripped her shoulders as the waves approached, then the huge wave, roaring and engulfing them, taking them down into the territory of the sea goddess, across the beautiful Eden on to a new beginning. His body relaxed, he opened his eyes, the fear had gone. He managed a broad satisfied grin. She did not grin back. She didn't need to. She too had laid to rest the old, and underneath an almond tree, had gone into the new.

The Wet

Alison Campbell

She had his address smudged on recent postcards, so she knew he was still there. As she stepped into the dazzling light from the comfort of the smoke-windowed bus, she took in the fierce wads of casuarinas and frangipanis and the moist warmth of the sea air. It was not yet the wet season.

She felt small. Not small as you would in the city, where the height and volume of buildings swoop over you crushing your eyeballs, but physically made small by the giant blue sky and the light, white box buildings wavering along the edge of the land. They were clinging there for a time, unsure for how long. The cyclone some years ago had, after all, got rid of the last lot. Scraggy squat bushes clawed into the dry earth of the promenade road. Palms, wispy like balding heads, nodded.

Walking along the wide mall, rucksack on her back, she savoured the occasional blast of delicious coolness from the air-conditioned shops. People walked slower here. Not measured, but ambling. Nearly all wore sarongs or shorts. The government buildings launched skyward, looking over wide streets with cars diagonally parked.

She wondered if Tam would live in a tropical house too, with banana plants and a rotary sprinkler in the garden teasing rust tufts into grass again. She knew he'd be pleased to see her, an old friend from the homeland, from the past. She'd written as soon as she'd arrived in the country, never realising how long it would take to journey the 2500 miles up the coast.

'Bussing and hitching my way up,' she'd written. 'Planning to fly back home after getting the fare together – by Christmas. Is this realistic? See you soon, Ellen.'

Stuart Crescent wasn't wide like the centre of town, but it was quiet, overlooking a patchy park area. Tam's flat was over the drive-in wine shop. She climbed the stone staircase and came to two neat buff doors protected by fly screens. Number three was the one to the left of the bannisters.

Ellen had been at Tam's flat exactly one week when the job came up; housemaid at Casuarina Beach Motel.

'Take it,' said Tam. 'Get work while you can, you might not want to be here till Christmas.'

'What d'you mean?' said Ellen, wrinkling up her nose as she wiped the white zinc protector off.

'They say the weather's going to break late this year. From now on it gets hotter and fiercer by the day . . . and with your colouring . . .'

Ellen began to recalculate. But no, she'd not have her fare home till Christmas. It was that simple. She bought more large tubs of zinc protector and borrowed Tam's straw hat for when he worked on the pineapple farms. She wore it permanently, apart from when she was at the motel.

The five a.m. start was the best bit. She enjoyed walking down towards the beach in the cool, unswept mornings, in the not-quite dawn, tables to set, trays to arrange for room service. The break-fast room was vast, like a ballroom. It opened on to a white patio with miniature palms in brass boxes and an oval swimming pool.

Businessmen used the hotel. She got used to seeing government officials striding around in socks and shorts. If they accompanied the men at all, women wore strappy towelling dresses in bright colours and looked overtanned and unattainable.

Two weeks into the job a delegation from the Aboriginal Land Rights came for lunch. She felt embarrassed by all the petty etiquette rules she had to adhere to; always serving the vegetables from the right and standing back while the wine was tasted. She shuffled awkwardly waiting for the verdict.

'Good grog.'

She felt crushed by this adherence to form which neither party wanted. In the kitchen, she snatched piles of meat from the Bain Marie, and, shoving it on a silver ashet, thrust it into the middle of their table. She felt it was the least she could do.

A routine was set up where neither she nor Tam intruded too much into the other's life. She returned from work at 2.30 p.m., showered and lay down on the mattress set at right angles to the television. The fan whirled above her and the occasional cockroach crinkled the garbage bag in the corner.

The pattern was broken by an acquaintance of Tam's, who invited him to dinner. When she knew he had a friend staying, she asked Ellen too. It was the carpet which surprised Ellen the most.

'My southern indulgence and inheritance,' Gill explained. It was soft and long as sheepskin and very white. All over the house. It was the first time Ellen had seen a carpet since she'd arrived here.

After marinated steaks and a green salad, they lay in the garden in the relative cool of the evening. Gill and Tam talked as if they were old friends, and Ellen lay looking at the inky sky. Banana plants grew to one side of the house and sunflowers jostled the bamboo. She would never get used to the mosquitos.

From the top of the spiral stairs which led to the back of the house, a neat brown head appeared.

'Hi,' it said.

'Ellen, meet Roger the Lodger,' trilled Gill, and rolled over till she bumped hips with Tam.

In bed that night, Ellen again stared up, this time at the spangle of Dayglo stars on the ceiling.

'They're supposed to be in the shape of Orion,' said Roger whose name was really Don.

He had told Ellen he was up here to get over his marriage. He said he phoned his daughter twice a week and made her a tape every Sunday . . . songs, stories, nonsense. Her name was Sammy and he felt very much in love with her. Ellen asked him a little about his old life in Sydney. He'd worked there, then travelled to Indonesia to work some more. Sammy had been born there. Ellen wondered if he felt very lonely living up here, light years from family life, with 'the delectable Gill' as Tam called her. Don said he was just biding his time up here trying to get used to the heat. Maybe when the wet came he'd be able to think clearer. Anyhow, he reckoned he'd be up here another year.

He rubbed her arm softly with his wizened fingers. His face was small, features neat and symmetrical with sun lines crackling round his cheeks and chin. His light green eyes looked washed out from too much harsh sun. When dressed, his clothes were curiously formal. Washable fawn trousers with fake seams running down the fronts and a white shirt with button-down collar.

'Do you want to go back to your daughter?' Ellen asked after breakfast next morning.

'Yep. But I don't think my wife would have me.' He poured another coffee and brushed the croissant crumbs neatly from the table to the pedal bin.

He's an ideal lodger all right, thought Ellen. Always clearing up. She had the feeling Gill liked it that way too. She came in at that moment wearing a peach kimono, her hair just washed, slapping down her shoulders. With her glasses off, Gill's eyes were large, like Tam's, and danced restlessly from side to side when she talked or listened. Ellen felt vaguely devoured.

'Well, you two look as though you've had a good time here,' she said smiling at the table but meaning the bedroom.

'What about having a barbie later?' she said.

Don said, 'Great.' He stood, wiping crumbs off his hands. He seemed unused to invitations.

Gill drove controlled and fast. Ellen wondered how Tam could sit so easily beside her not seeming to see the twists in the road. She sat tensely at the back arching her feet on invisible brakes under the cover of the seat. Don rested his hand on hers and smiled out of the window.

Fifty miles or so was no distance to go for a barbecue out here, Gill assured her. Powerful shoulders strung back, her arms thrust forward grasping the wheel she looked like some kind of galleon figurehead, as the slipstream whipped strands of hair from her plait. For their benefit in the back she spoke deliberately loud, turning round to flash smiles and make eye contact. Ellen wished she wouldn't.

They turned off and drove for an hour along an increasingly bumpy track with a middle line of short scrub. Potholes completed the defeat of the bitumen.

'Look. Right.' Gill flapped a hand. Ellen stared at the thick clump of water buffalo pounding the scrub. They reached the rock. Gill slammed the boot with a crack that momentarily sliced the hanging stillness. A dark bird wheeled. Obiri, like a huge sentinel, hunched before them.

After they had carried the equipment and Eskies out, Ellen walked to the rock. She pored over the drawings on its face. Fish with visible skeletons, zigzag tracks, X-ray kangaroos. She lost sense of time.

'Come and get it,' Gill's voice zoomed in on her thoughts. Ellen turned and saw Gill tossing meat on the charcoal, lifting her face to the scent like an animal after prey. Ellen walked over, reluctant to leave the void her mind had dived into, but hungry all the same.

Too hot and unsheltered to sprawl in the open, they crouched in the shadow of an opened car door, scrubby spinifex catching bare-legs as they moved.

'Not a place to run out of petrol,' Tam observed, glancing at the sitting landscape. The sky hung around them in a circle.

'Or water,' said Don. But Ellen felt sure he would be able to lead them to a cactus and draw sap with a penknife. The noise of a high string being twanged followed a shrill whistle.

'Whipbird,' said Gill, pushing the hammock of her skirt further down to protect her calves and licking meat juice from her broad fingers, one by one.

'We could go for a swim on the way back,' said Tam, as they turned on to the main track again. He had his flagon of Barossa Valley between his knees. He refilled plastic glasses, making sure he had a hand free to hold Gill's after she changed gear.

She was driving faster now. Night would come down like a hood. Dusk here was as fleeting as the nostalgic memory of it back home. They would not be going for a swim, Ellen knew. She could see Gill needed to get back. She felt Don's body beside her like a safety net. Something about his preoccupation with his daughter made her feel more secure with him.

She felt, looking at Gill and Tam, that they were like hungry animals prowling past each other. Who would be first to pounce? Swim abandoned, they rested, panting in the heat of the garden. They'd divided into pairs again. Don laced his fingers in Ellen's.

'You should be able to see the Southern Cross on nights like these,' he said.

'Why not now?' said Ellen.

'Maybe the wet's going to break,' he said.

Ellen felt increasingly locked in by the heat. It was like waiting for something to crack. Her walks to work seemed to take longer than ever. The motel seemed like a mirage, shimmering against the Timor Sea. The air also vibrated with a radiance that pierced. The sea, like mercury, did not seem wet. Bitumen roads roasted her thongs, and nibbled the plastic to a fray.

She showered three times a day and still felt it was not enough. At Tam's, she insisted they had the fan on full all night. Tam said she'd regret it when the bills came.

'With any luck I won't be here then,' was Ellen's first thought. She flipped through her bank book. 'But I'll have to be. Seven weeks to Christmas and I'm still only at Dubai.' She'd taken to calculating the rate of her journey home against her savings.

The weather broke on a Saturday. They were inside Gill's house, her three fans whirring the clingy humidity in unison above them, a synchronised dance of blades. Gill drank lime and soda cocktails laced with gin in a belled glass, the rim frosted in sugar. She lay on her back, legs resting on a chair. Tam lazed beside her drinking determindly on a six pack.

Don sat at the kitchen table drawing a picture for Sammy, his only concession to the humidity, a cotton pair of shorts, instead of full length trousers. Ellen lolled her head against a cushion. The headphones of the stereo weighed her head down. She wanted to sink on to the carpet beside Gill. Her ears opened to the windchime sounds of Don's tape; fluted gamelan music he had recorded in Indonesia. The unfamiliar rhythms fluttered and startled her inside. The high flute notes spun while deeper resonant gongs rippled and dived underneath.

Ellen wanted to move her body like a snake round the room to the music, to weave in and out of the chairs, to glide round the table to press her body on the carpet and move her arms strongly against the weave, in arched serpent-like movements.

But she had no energy. The heat and stillness had absorbed it through these last weeks. She felt claimed by it. She wiped her hands again on the thick cotton armrest covers. She would have to leave before Christmas after all, before she had saved her full fare. She'd get to, perhaps, Southern Turkey . . . Ellen thought she'd just have to hitch from there.

Anything would be better than this . . . a permanent cascade of sweat, heat-induced migraines which threatened to make her brains explode. Ellen looked at the door, closed to keep out the heat. Through its glass panelling there seemed to be movement. She saw the leaves of the palm trees change direction sharply as though whipped. Like signals they rose and sliced the sky in one unified upward sweep. Behind, the sky gathered itself. Drained to lilac, it now flooded in to a deep boiling pea green.

Gill heaved herself upright. She and Tam went to the door where Don now stood. Suddenly the door was rushed open by the wind and Ellen felt a huge oven rush of air moving at her. Gill turned towards her, eyes wide, mouthing something at her. She obviously thought Ellen could hear her 'The wet, the wet,' she was saying.

Ellen, headphones still in place waved her words away . . .' I know, I know, the sweat.' She couldn't take it anymore.

Suddenly Gill lifted her arms above her head and peeled off her top. She disappeared through the door in what looked like a parachute dive, although Ellen thought afterwards she must almost have slid down the stairway. Tam grabbed a can and rushed after her. Don had already gone.

Ellen sat up. Did she sense change? She smelled the air. Her neck felt it the keenest. It had stopped wanting to roll her head away. Instead, it felt like a fine stalk of bamboo perched ready to blow where the wind and took it. The rain started. It plummeted finely from the sky at first, then in dense shrouds. No fine European drizzle this. It was a fist of wet; a deluge from nowhere. Straining against the headphones cord, Ellen stood at the door and looked down on the garden.

Her orange sarong sticking to her like a body stocking, Gill slid and glided round the now slippery lawn in ever widening circles. She was bare to the waist. With her hair plastered to her breasts she looked like some exuberant large bird, desperate for flight. Her eyes were closed, her mouth in a big 'O'. Tam, prancing like some ungainly pierrot bounded behind her pausing only to throw his head back and pour lager into the rain already coursing down his body.

On the balcony Ellen watched this bizarre mime show, before turning towards Don in the corner of the garden. For Ellen he was centre stage and she stared at him. He was lying spreadeagled on his back. Beside him, his shorts, pants and shirt were folded, a careful, sodden pile. Don's mouth was open. Ellen could see his throat moving rhythmically as he drank the rain. He looked like some pale fish who'd just claimed his pond again.

Ellen removed the headphones. A peal of thunder cracked and slammed at her ears instead, but the fragile gamelan still rang inside her, as she picked her way down the glistening spiral steps to the lawn. The rain soaked her by the time she reached the bottom step. She was instantly revived. She was going to stay on till Christmas after all, and, right now she was going to show Don her snake dance.

The Boot Shop Sisters

Sylvia Fair

Christmas 1920 proved an out-and-out flop for the infant daughters of Mary and Emrys Jones, High Class Footwear. For on Christmas Eve who should arrive but Aunt Haulwen. Without a word she whisked all three nieces through the benumbed streets of Pantiog to her cottage on the outskirts: then on Boxing Day whisked all three back to the Boot Shop.

Home again, the girls found their mother confined to bed, a fire lit in the bedroom grate, her Sunday slippers resting upside down under the wash-stand.

Their father, next to the bed, looked totally out of place in his severe suit and brogues – although he smiled benignly enough when his daughters entered.

Their mother smiled too, propped to a sitting position with two fat frilly pillows at her back, in her arms a white bundle the younger girls took to be a third fat frilly pillow until it let out a long, thin mewl. Sarah, the oldest, who knew a human baby when she heard one, approached the bed and stood tiptoe.

'Is that ours?'

Their mother nodded. 'Your new sister. Isn't she a doll?'

She turned the pillowy parcel round to show the face – as unlike a doll's as could be imagined.

'Ginger hair?' observed Poll, deciding not to mention the wrinkles.

Daisy, baby of the family until now, felt the need to test the truth of all this. 'So what's her name?' she challenged.

'Christmas,' both parents said at once, with such snap precision Daisy half expected them to link pinkies and make a wish.

'It doesn't sound a regular name to me, Christmas doesn't,' said Sarah.

Mr Jones seemed glad she'd noticed. He buttoned his jacket a notch. 'Well, she's hardly a regular baby, is she? To be born on Christmas Day is rather special.'

'Special beyond telling,' cooed Mrs Jones, giving Baby Christmas a tweak to the chin, 'aren't you, my pixie?' Then, despite the severity of the weather outside and the snow-covered mountain tops, she unwrapped the lower end of the white flannelette parcel and untied crocheted chains belonging to two small bootees. 'There! Did you ever see a daintier set of tootsies?'

Daisy stared at the baby's feet, amazed. Not a chilblain to be seen!

Frost bit hard that night. The girls snuggled down, all three in the one feather bed, noses frozen, swollen toes fondling the scorching hot-water bottle they shared. Daisy alone kept her feet to herself, nursing a heel-blister the size of a half-crown. Unable to work her aunt's unwieldy button-hook this afternoon, and with Aunt Haulwen unwilling to wait for slowcoaches, she'd had no choice but to hobble home behind the others, buttons undone, boots flapping. At least the soreness took her mind off the new baby to some degree.

'I propose,' said Sarah, her voice muffed under the blankets, 'that we refuse to call her Christmas.'

'So what do we call her instead?' asked Poll in the darkness.

'Bunty.'

In an age rife with rehashed names, when at the drop of a hat a Mary could become a Poll, a Margaret a Daisy, who would argue?

'It's Bunty, then,' Poll approved.

'*Anything*'s better than *Christmas*,' Daisy agreed, and Bob's your uncle! The motion was carried.

As Sarah made headway promoting the favoured name; as Poll watched the wispy hair ripen to a copper blaze; as Daisy kept an eye open for blemishes on those dimpled feet, baby sister Bunty outgrew her crocheted bootees. The following Christmas she stood upright, later learned to walk wearing two-toned brown kid shoes with buttoned T-strap. Not once was Bunty lumbered with her sisters' cast-offs, Daisy noticed. From the age of four Mr Jones gave his special daughter the pick of the shop as birthday-cum-Christmas present, and for her first winter boots she chose the best: patent leather and white calfskin, four buttons down one side and a silk tassle at the ankle.

Sarah and Poll continued to be palmed off with surplus stock, using up lines that didn't sell. While Daisy slopped about in hand-me-downs – maid's shoes several sizes too large – Poll and Sarah tottered on cuban-heeled lace-ups in shades no one else wanted, or crowded their toes into imitation lizard-skins, a fad that failed to catch fire with Pantiogians. Feeling on a par with the original Ugly Sisters they watched as Bunty, blind to their martyrdom, trifled with shoes of the most fanciful styles; silver tinsel sandals one season, cream satin dancing pumps the next. 'Are they comfy, my pet?' her mother would ask each time she tried out a new pair.

'Not that she has all the privileges,' Sarah reminded Poll. 'At least Dad has more sense than to trust that flibbertigibbet with the job of breaking in.'

Poll nodded. It took a fair amount of stamina, pacing the lino'd passage for a prescribed number of hours in stiff shoes – an exclusive service offered to regular customers whose own tender feet balked at new leather.

Such vanity! thought Poll, catching Bunty blatantly admiring the tilt of one foot as she sat. Poll couldn't begin to count the hours Bunty sat massaging her precious tootsies, or else bathing them in aromatic oils, manicuring the nails, wriggling toes supple as indiarubber.

Aghast at such extravagances Sarah, Poll and Daisy veered towards frugality in the hopes of showing her up. Their sacrifice went unapplauded.

'Not a scrap of humility in her,' Poll said, 'and as for her hair! What she puts on it I can only imagine, but I tell you this as gospel. At the Girl Guides' Garden Party Vicar Thomas had to put his sunglasses on when she went to stand in front of him.'

'She'll go to seed,' Sarah predicted, 'you'll see. People born looking like dolls are the first to show wear.'

Though Poll refused to accept that Bunty started off anything like, she had to admit that her youngest sister looked every inch the doll now, a rubber doll with too much bounce in her stride and no wonder, with feet so well catered for, swanking down the road in crêpe-de-Chine courts, multicoloured wedges, peep-toes, slingbacks – all within the space of a few months!

'And all she ever *does* in those fancy shoes is dance with soldiers in the Drill Hall on a Saturday night.'

It neither astonished nor upset the boot shop sisters when Bunty ran off with a soldier of the Polar Bear regiment billeted in Pantiog for the winter, Lloyd's Bank having been turned into barracks for the duration. Light sleepers swore they heard the clop of her wartime clogs proceeding westwards down Police Station Pitch at five in the morning, heading for the railway, sure as eggs. Scorning the poster asking IS YOUR JOURNEY REALLY NECESSARY? she bought a one-way ticket to Newport via Tal-y-llyn, never to set foot in Pantiog for the next fifty years.

The shock of her daughter's abrupt departure, coming so close after her husband's untimely death (not from bombs, for none fell squarely on any market town in mid-Wales, but from suffocation by a rogue parachute while roving the hills) put Mrs Jones in bed for life. She went into a serious decline, her outdoor shoes closeted for good. Now she depended on her stay-at-home daughters to pander to her needs as well as running the shop on her behalf.

Wartime scarcities forced the girls to carry lines that would have made their father pop-eyed with disbelief. Alongside utility wear stamped CC41 they now sold bottles of liquid stockings and home-made jewellery as accessories: beechnuts and seashells painted gold and silver, with broochpin attached. They put their runaway sister's shoes on display marked SHOP SOILED, generously reduced and without coupons. They could no longer afford to give away free laces with each pair sold; nor did they replace the last tin of Yardley's talc kept handy for customers in need of a puff before trying on, even though they'd had a glut of sweaty socked boys recently, wearing holey shoes with grubby insoles their mothers had cut from Quaker oat cardboard. Some parents ought to teach their children to look after their shoes.

Thanks to habits learned in infancy their own footwear had lasted well enough to be counted as museum pieces. *Feed the leather*, their father used to din into them, shoebrush in hand. *Never let an empty shoe stand on its own sole*. Throughout life, as though driven by supersitition, they turned their shoes upside down each night before bed so that the soles, facing the ceiling, could breathe.

Now, Christmases passed by almost unobserved. As mother wilted upstairs, frequently calling out for her baby to come home, Poll in the back kitchen fried whale-meat sausages on the gas stove; Sarah concocted Dress-Shoe Blacking following an old recipe, using gum Arabic and treacle, vinegar, ink and spirit, mixing the whole to a smooth paste with powdered tragacanth to bind it. She intended putting the finished product under the counter, to sell only to customers with the wit to bring an empty Cherry Blossom tin to put the stuff in.

'Don't you dare slam that door!' shrieked Daisy, sitting at the table counting out yesterday's clothing coupons, piling them up in tiny stacks so flimsy she hardly dared breathe herself.

Mrs Jones hung on to life by the toenails right until the new year of 1947.

'Keep your father's business going, there's good girls,' she begged with her dying breath.

They buried her behind the Presbyterian Chapel next to Mr Jones, or possibly on top, space being at a premium these days – in the nick of time, too. For on January 26th came the blizzards. Soon, twenty-foot drifts blocked every road leading to Pantiog and froze solid over the chapel yard. For eight weeks the railway provided the sole link with the world; and after a fortnight of such fierce storms not a decent boot could be had for love nor money.

The boot shop sisters wisely stayed indoors. They served in the shop wearing overcoats, their feet zipped into brown suede ankle boots, Morleys, built to last. Winter over, they oiled the zips and sprinkled crystals inside to stop the lambswool from matting; then they put them away.

A cemetery planned for the northern end of the town promised to relieve crammed graveyards. Sarah, Poll and Daisy, excited by the prospect, took walks to the site every Thursday afternoon when the shop was shut, to monitor progress. They proceeded more slowly than they once did, mindful of Daisy's feet, Poll's hip, Sarah's back. In their youth, each had unthinkingly adopted a gait to minimise the twinge of a corn or the ache of a hammer-toe, or to disperse the pins-and-needles of fallen arches. A shift of posture was all it took to bring instant relief. It also caused havoc in hidden areas: the slow erosion of a hip joint, a distressed back muscle.

Sarah had acquired a stoop of late. Poll leaned more heavily on her rubber-tipped walking-stick. Daisy, finding prolonged contact with hard paving stones gave her bunions gyp, would every now and then take a trot to lighten pressure, then slow down and wait for Poll and Sarah, so that people in Pantiog began to call her Daisy Trot-a-bit.

Often, a needle-like pang would shoot up from an instep, to register on the face, and another crease would deepen a fraction. Still they plodded on, heading for the cemetery, eyeing the shoes of passersby, finding it rare, now, to hear a shoe creak, but when one did Sarah could be guaranteed to say, 'Well, we know who hasn't paid for *his* shoes, don't we, girls?'

They reached the cemetery and, as always, stopped to look over the new gate.

'The scope of the place!' Poll marvelled. 'It should last for centuries. All that trim grass just waiting to be dug up.'

Then, as always on a Thursday afternoon, they pondered over who, of all the likely candidates in Pantiog, might be first in.

As it turned out, that honour went to Aunt Haulwen who died aged ninety-two. It fell upon her only nieces to buy a plot and settle up. Sarah thought it might be wise, while they were at it, to buy plots for themselves.

'Three plots, or four?' asked Daisy.

'Better make it four,' Sarah decided. 'Because she'll be back, you can bet your great-granny's Welsh dresser. Everyone comes home to Pantiog in the end. That's why the graveyards are overflowing. That's why it's common sense to book in here early.'

Sarah reached retirement age, and still Bunty hadn't turned up. As thick as triplets now, Poll and Daisy decided to call it a day too. They felt out of joint with trends in the footwear trade, the speed of turnover in fashion enough to put anyone in a tizzy. Men expected square-toed slip-ons one minute, winkle-pickers the next.

The sisters sold off all the remaining stock at half price. They told travellers not to call any more, then draped a green plush curtain across the empty shop window. That done, they retreated to a back room, their horny feet pushed deep inside tartan woollen slippers with sponge soles and teddy bear buttons.

They looked at the clock on the mantelpiece more often than they needed to, for they had no set routine; it was as if Bunty had given them a time, and any minute she might be home. They'd listen for the rattle of the shop door, the only access to their living quarters, and shake their heads when it turned out to be nothing.

When they ventured out, they went together, wearing their stalwarts: Poll in black leather monk's shoes with buckled strap, Sarah in moccasins, Daisy in Clarks sandals stretched to accommodate her ever-growing Spanish onions. So that when the prodigal returned she found her sisters in the very same footwear they'd worn when she left home.

Daisy answered the rattle at the shop door this time. She recognised her little sister by the hair, still a copper blaze, if tinged with henna. 'Hey, girls!' she called into the house; then, deeming it more respectful to use the proper name for once, whooped: 'Christmas has come!' which brought Sarah and Poll running, thinking Daisy had stolen a march on them and gone senile out of turn.

All three stared agog at Bunty's hair, and at her complexion, soft as Hush Puppy suede and without a wrinkle. Their eyes sneaked downwards next, to her feet. They might have guessed. Immaculate and springy in natty red shoes neat as the day they'd been bought.

Bunty stared back at her sisters, their faces, like their shoes, still recognisable despite crazing and sagging of the hide: their hair too, faded pale as thistledown but in a style unchanged since wartime when a roll of hair right round the head, tucked into elastic, was thought to be most fetching.

This time, Bunty had journeyed the last lap by Post Bus from the nearest town still boasting a railway. Although empty handed apart from a pension book her sisters welcomed her home, and made room for her, installing her in the bedroom she'd been born in.

Twice a week she painted her toe-nails, choosing whatever colour took her fancy. The sister, their faces furrowed like those of the three bull mastiffs kept to guard the tannery once, said nothing. But the truth was, Bunty and her feet gave them the goat. She talked about little else. She positively pranced about the place, swanky as ever. She went so far as to claim that some high-flown chiropodist had been sweet on her. He'd been known to mention her feet in his lectures at medical conferences all over the world. He'd also written about them in *The Lancet*.

'Believe that,' Sarah warned, 'and you'll believe anything.'

'Wonder what happened to her soldier?' said Daisy.

They'd noticed the lack of a wedding ring, so supposed she hadn't stuck him for long.

'Those Polar Bears got drafted to the desert, didn't they, along with Monty's 8th Army? Maybe he went with them and never came back.'

The thought quite saddened Daisy, gifted with a sentimental streak. How did soldiers march across oceans of fine sand, she wondered, in those heavy boots? She worried about it so long that, asleep in her armchair, she dreamed of an endless trail of hobnail boots right across the Sahara . . .

Why Bunty took it into her head to climb into the loft that Tuesday afternoon in late November, none of them could be sure.

Perhaps hoping to track down her collection of shoes? The crash as she fell through an upstairs ceiling quite unnerved them, snoozing in the back room. The fall did Bunty's precious feet no good at all.

'You can rest assured, dear,' whispered Daisy, doing a stint at the injured's bedside and realising the seriousness of the mishap. 'Sarah had the presence of mind, bless her, to book you in at the new cemetery. There's a comfortable plot all ready and waiting. No overcrowding, like at the chapel.'

Injuries or no injuries, Bunty sat upright in bed. 'I am not going to be *buried*!'

Her order came out like a bark. It seemed to Daisy that each word had been scraped from the depths of a near-empty barrel inside her ribs.

'I have willed my body to medical science, so there,' she went on. 'On account of my remarkable feet. The entire world will benefit from the research. There's an envelope on the mantelpiece. It's all arranged.'

Then, exhausted from her outburst, she sank back into the pillows.

'Most noble, I'm sure,' said Daisy, thinking of white-coated doctors going to all that bother, picking away with their forceps, pulling at sinews, only to find Bunty's feet built along the same lines as everyone else's.

Bunty died on Christmas Day, seventy years old almost to the minute. Her sisters were beside themselves, an everyday funeral distressing enough – but *this*! On Christmas Day too?

In the buff envelope on the mantelpiece in Bunty's bedroom they had found the so-called will, an official-looking document not easy to make head or tail of, with two numbers to ring urgently in the event, the second number for out-of-hours calls. A vehicle would be sent immediately to take delivery, it promised.

'So her feet must have been special!' said Daisy, round-eyed.

'Poppycock,' said Sarah.

With the out-of-hours telephone number safe inside Sarah's coat pocket, the three of them walked the quiet streets to the phone box. They crowded into it. They'd had no reason to use a phone since the days of operators. They stared at the instructions, mystified. It took all three to work out the push buttons and money-slot, and how on earth did a person get her money back without a Button B to press? Only they need not have worried; they didn't have a reclaim any money. A voice answered.

Sarah spoke loudly into the mouthpiece, as if phoning somewhere as far afield as Cardiff required extra volume. Then she listened, her ear so tightly pressed against the earpiece her sisters could not hear a thing. At last she replaced the receiver, missing the hook twice before managing to lodge the wretched contraption.

'You got through all right?' asked Daisy nervously.

Sarah pushed open the kiosk door and led the way out into the nippy north wind.

'Short staffed until after the New Year holiday,' she said with some satisfaction. 'And after that there's a go-slow. They can't foresee a time when they could take delivery.'

'You mean, they don't want her feet?' asked Poll. 'And her with such highfalutin ideas? It just goes to show! It doesn't do to die on Christmas Day.'

'They said we must make other arrangements,' said Sarah.

'So she'll have to be buried like everyone else?' said Daisy. 'Feet and all?'

'Like everyone else.'

'Well, I must say,' said Poll. 'That's cut her down to size. High time too.'

'Good job we made provision, is all I can say,' said Daisy. 'Where to now, Sarah?'

'To Ben Lewis the undertaker.'

United in their private rejoicings they set off, willing to interrupt Ben Lewis' Christmas goose, if needs be. Back down the street they strode, their step sprightly despite their many ailments, all three thankful to have matters back on a proper footing.

The Fireproof Lady

Eleanor Dare

Sat: Annual Christmas fair.
Sun: Public worship, the minister Frank Turner.
Tue: Women's Guild coffee morning.
Fri: Midnight Carol service, flute recital by Luke Turner.

Before I met him you could say I was lonely as a bastard on Father's Day. Luke Turner. He's a vain little tart. Piss elegant. Reckons he's got the biggest dick this side of the M25.

I've never been interested in dicks. I'm what teachers like to call a lone wolf. The solitary type. These teachers reckon they know everything about us, but they know fuck all – take Luke, half of them reckon he's the flute playing angel, and the other half imagine we're knocking each other off. You know, teenage sweethearts. Puke.

I knew it from the first moment I saw him at the fifth form induction, he had it written across his forehead like a neon tatoo – SCPO – Suspiciously Cute, Probably Queer. Of all the other people in the world only the Forest Hill Skins seem to have caught on, they like to chase us down Dartmouth Road yelling out 'POOFTERS!' I don't reckon a girl can be called a poof though – it's a semantic error, a misnomer if you like. Still, what can you expect from a bunch of Tipp-Ex trippers? Anyway, Luke reckons they only do it because they fancy him. Luke is to vanity what nuns are to self-effacement.

It's this vanity of his that nearly got us done over last Christmas. That and the flute case. The flute case and the lighter fuel and Luke Turner's vanity.

'Hello Eddie love, come into the warm,' said Mrs Turner. It was Christmas Eve, for some reason she had purple tinsel in her hair.

Mrs Turner met my father once, ever since then she's taken it upon herself to feel sorry for me. Luke says I should milk it for all it's worth – ie try and get her to make us more cups of tea. That evening Mrs Turner leant over and kissed me as I came in, leaving a light sprinkling of flesh-coloured powder and the shadow of a flush on my frozen cheeks.

'He's upstairs, as you can hear.' Selfish bastard had The Human League on full volume.

'Don't worry Mrs Turner, I'll turn it down.' It was a creepy thing to say, but in those days I didn't know the difference between affection and sex – not having a mother and all that, the kiss temporarily phased me.

'That bitch told you to turn it down!' Luke screamed, leaping up from the dressing table and turning the hi-fi back up to maximum volume. As you can tell, he's a total shitebag. A fact much camouflaged by Vivien Leigh eyes and a cupid's bow mouth with a margarine wouldn't melt in it innocent-boy grin.

'Up your knackered old bum!' I screamed in return, wrenching the wretched record off the turntable and flinging it out of the bedroom window, always open ajar to waft away the incriminating Marlboro fumes. Well, it was luscious seeing 'Don't You Want Me Baby' fractured into a thousand tiny pieces, and after Luke had given me one of his dead arm jobs we pissed ourselves looking down on the front garden carnage, lighting up a couple of high tar cigs.

'I've told them,' said Luke, tipping back a bottle of Woodpecker cider. 'If I don't get a Sony Walkman – SONY mark you – if it isn't in my hands by ten o'clock tomorrow morning, that's it. I'm leaving. If it hasn't got an anti-hiss button I'm suing the bastards AND I'm trashing their poxy Renault Five.'

The word 'poxy' hit a vicious high note resembling the screech of fingernails against a school blackboard. It bounced off the ceiling rose, immediately muffled by the bombsite debris all over his bedroom floor. Luke's room looks like one of those after a prison riot scene you see on the nine o'clock news, all that's missing are the shit stains over the walls and a government inquiry.

'What about you love?' he drew on his cigarette like Lauren Bacall, with the high cheekbones and everything. 'What's it to be this year – another pair of thermonuclear Derry boots?'

'Thermolactycal,' I corrected him, 'God, what a nightmare, I've told the old git I'm a Sunni Muslim these days and he shouldn't bother.'

'That was a mistake,' said Luke, swinging back on his chair in the traditionally forbidden fashion. 'You could've gone for hard cash.'

'This is my father we're talking about,' I said. 'The crap or nothing man.'

The chair creaked ominously but didn't actually break. 'The man with the opposite Midas touch,' said Luke, 'everything he touches turns into a turd.'

'Wish I'd been swopped at birth.'

'Parents,' said Luke, 'what a bunch of cunts.'

'If only,' I said.

The stench of smouldering mince pies drove us out of the house. Just as we were going down the garden path, treading over the chips of vinyl, Luke's mum came rushing out.

'Don't forget your flute love,' she said, adding 'I didn't hear you practice.'

'Oh for fuck's sake,' snapped Luke. Whenever he spoke to her in those days an infinity of rage seemed to well up from inside him, I didn't understand it. It seemed, well . . . unreasonable.

Mrs Turner ignored the remark and handed him the thin black case. 'Have a nice time Eddie, see you later on.'

The whole of Forest Hill smelt like a giant mincepie.

'Your mother is a saint,' I said as we walked down Sunderland Road, immediately tipping Luke into one of his half-arsed rages.

'Just because you fancy her, and don't think I don't know about it.'

'You bad tempered old poof.'

'Diesel dyke.'

All the tired old Christmas lights were flinching on and off in the crappy shop windows, blinking between adverts for Silk Cut and Rothmans. The last few Christmases I noticed how the excitement had worn off. Now it felt like an excuse for your family to get you in a corner. Drive you into captivity as it were.

'We'll nip in here for a drink,' Luke announced as we approached the imposing bulk of The Telegraph pub. He said it dead casual, like it was no big deal. As if the landlord wasn't this notorious psychopath who could sniff out an underage drinker from 500 yards. Looking back on it, ordering two lagers with blackcurrant was probably what gave the game away, I suppose Luke thought the blackcurrant bit would lessen the offence. Whilst he was ordering the drinks I practised a few of my lighter tricks – filling my hand up with gas then flicking at the flint to cause a miniature but harmless explosion in the palm of my hand.

I got the idea for it from this book about human freaks that Luke kept under the bed along with all his cowboy orgy literature; in it there was this neat picture of a fireproof lady thrusting her arm into a tongue of flame and washing her hands in boiling lead with absolutely no side effects. I'd been perfecting a few of my own stunts recently – on good days I could pluck up enough courage to fill my mouth with lighter fuel and ignite it, which had a spectacularly disturbing effect upon anyone who witnessed it at the right moment.

That night the pub was filled to capacity with middle-aged creeps in car coats. A couple of them saw my hand on fire and looked gratifyingly alarmed. Luke came over with the strange looking drinks. 'After I've perfected the flame eating I'm thinking of becoming a human cork.'

'Just think,' said Luke, panning out his hands like he could see my name in bright lights. 'You could be the first person to go UP the Niagara falls in a barrel.'

'YOU'RE OUT!' Boomed the voice of doom, silencing the entire pub.

Stone me – if it wasn't a six foot gorilla with a brain like an empty fertiliser sack.

'And a Happy Christmas to you too,' said Luke.

'Don't fucking cheek me.'

'If it's cheeks you want . . .' Luke batted his abundant eye lashes. Without further negotiation the outsized ape's arsehole picked up Luke's drink, kind of in slow motion, and tipped it with a zen-like calm straight over our Luke's ravishing head.

'I don't know what you're snickering at you bitch, you could have done something.'

'I was giving him one of my most withering stares.'

'You were gulping down your sodding pint.'

The passage that ran along beside the railway line was the sort of place adults always warned you about – one of those alleyways beloved of police reconstructions. Naturally it attracted us like a high-powered magnet, though on that occasion we went down it because Luke Shitepants didn't want to be seen on the high road looking like a wet rag. Understandable really, though entering the place was like passing through the valley of the shadow of death, with red blood dripping graffiti announcing FOREST HILL SKINS.

Being Christmas Eve there were no trains and certainly no commuters to speak of. The place stank of drunkards' piss and stand-up shagging. We pulled our jumper sleeves down over our hands and bowed our heads to the freezing wind. Broken glass crunched pleasingly under our twin pairs of Monkey boots.

'One day Father Christmas goes to a psychiatrist,' said Luke, swinging the flute case as we walked. 'Dr, Dr – you've got to help me, it's too awful' . . . 'What's the problem Mr Claus?' the shrink says, and Father Christmas breaks down sobbing – 'I no longer believe in myself.'

'I've had that problem all my life,' I said.

On the other side of a sagging chain-link fence we walked passed the ends of ramshackle back gardens, tangled with undergrowth and moulding mattresses. This was Forest Hill's equivalent of the Bohemian quarter, or so we imagined. Most of the big old houses were occupied by squatters – arty types, students, clapped-out hippies clinging on to the seventies. Drug dealers, ecology party members, serial killers – our imaginations ran riot. It was comforting to glimpse the odd bit of Christmas decoration within the lit-up bowls of these decaying structures. High up in an attic room someone was playing a Marc Almond record – 'Say Hello, Wave Goodbye', Luke sang along to it.

'Don't look now,' I said, then added 'It's all right – I thought it was Todger and the bootboys.'

'Nah,' said Luke.

Two men came towards us, emerging through the night-time dinginess. They were both carrying brown beer bottles, staggering in cheap bomber jackets and stretch jeans that made their legs look fat. We moved to one side to let them pass.

'Happy Christmas,' Luke mumbled.

'What was that?' said the tallest one, flushed with a fresh crop of acne. Rapidly the expression on his drunken face passed through a series of transformations, beginning with harmless oblivion and ending in unmistakeable menace.

'What did you say cunt?'

'He said "Happy Chistmas", that's all,' I said, my heart trying to beat its way out of my rib cage.

'And what are you – a He, a She, or an It?'

All I could do was gulp for more air, suddenly there wasn't enough of it. The smaller man had done a complete circle around us, blocking our only escape route.

'What's in the case then – snooker cue?'

'It's a flute,' said Luke, almost inaudible.

'Oh – a "flute",' the tall one put on a snobby accent as if he were imitating Luke, though Luke never said it in a posh voice.

'Mummy and Daddy buy it for you? Let's have a tune.'

'It's too cold,' said Luke. 'It's got to warm up.'

Suddenly the big one was right in Luke's face. Luke instinctively drew back so he was flat against the corrugated iron that guarded the railway line.

'You're Queer.' The words were spat out so viciously that the heat from his mouth appeared in clouds, like hate made visible.

'They're both fucking queer,' the other one said, swigging from his bottle. 'Queer as a fucking nine bob note, as my old man would say.'

'You can have the flute – take it.' Luke held the case out to him. He snatched it out of Luke's hands and tossed it effortlessly over the iron fence.

'That's what I think of your fucking queer flute.'

Luke backed even further into the fence like he wanted to merge himself into it. There was an odd pause, as if they expected us to instigate the next moment. Then, for the second time that night I saw things in slow motion – the arc of the taller man's arm as it rose with the bottle, the miserable look of eagerness in his dead grey eyes, Luke hunching into himself. The beer bottle inevitably smashing into the back of Luke's skull. And Luke crumpling under it, as if he had relaxed and gone with it's flow.

'You fucking BASTARD.' I heard the word bastard choking out of me like a high volume sob then found myself lashing out at him with my right hand, flicking my lighter into his pink skin – a spear of flame licking at those dead eyes.

'Jesus,' he gasped, covering them with his hands as the other man grabbed me from behind and threw me across the alley, so I hit the chain-link fence kind of bouncing up from it like an indoor wrestler, only the back of my head cracked against the newel post so I thought I was going to puke from it.

Luke staggered towards me, it seemed like a miracle that there was no blood on him, though his face was all bleached out and bloodless like a vampire's.

Then, just as we think our young lives are over – out of the starry night comes a big black labrador, bounding up to me and trying to lick my face – a labrador for Christ's sake. And this posh old geezer says 'What on EARTH is going on – don't you know it's Christmas?' Just like fucking Band Aid.

And the bastard's have disappeared. As if they had never been there in the first place.

Luke's giving me a leg up so I can climb over the fence and get his flute back. We're still shaking and the old man's gone tutting into the night like it's US that's done something wrong.

'Don't worry Luke, I'll get it back.' Luke's wheezing under me like a right old weed. 'Fat bitch,' he says.

There's a rush of wind out of Forest Hill station like Beelzebub farting in Hell – next minute the longest train you've ever seen in your life comes hurtling by at about 900 miles an hour, even so it takes six minutes for it to pass – all these ugly grey concrete containers and sinister square bits like nuclear waste trains. When it's gone there's no sign of the flute, only a weird clicking sound coming out of the rails.

'What do you want for Christmas Luke?' says Luke. 'Just a bottle over my head, a broken neck and my flute busted up.'

'You've got it!' I say, only I slip down and see Luke Turner is crying.

'Why does everybody hate us?' he asks, snorting the snot back up through his nose.

'They're jealous of your talent – your talent and your good looks.'

'You're right,' he sobs, feeling a little better. 'And they're jealous of you because you're my best friend.'

'Vain shitebag,' I say. But even though we're joking I get this dreadful feeling in the pit of my stomach, like life is a pile of shit.

We cross over the footbridge into Dacres Road, deciding to go and hide from the world in my house. Inside the Dietrich Bonhoffner church there's a midnight mass. We can see kids and families safe inside.

'Your Mum and Dad are going to think we've been murdered.'

'Good,' says Luke. 'It'll serve them right.'

Back home, my fat old bastard of a father has fallen asleep in front of the TV, bathing in the electric glow like a health treatment. I pull out the spare mattress and chuck a sleeping bag at Luke.

'Fuck Christmas,' he says. 'Fuck the carol service. Fuck Forest Hill.'

'Fuck everything,' I say.

'If I haven't got that Walkman I'll set fire to their house.'

We fell asleep fully clothed – bits of glass all over us, lager in Luke's hair. A taste like fresh blood in our mouths and the beginnings of twin bruises rising at the back of our heads. Luke fell asleep first, his perfectly formed mouth emitting a series of low snores. I dangled my arm over the side of the bed and gave him a punch, 'Fucking poof.'

'Diesel dyke,' he says in his sleep.

I must have fallen asleep some time after him – knowing Luke would never play a flute again – that my fire eating days were over.

Christmas in Croydon

Tara Rimsk

> Star light
> Star bright
> First star I see tonight
> I wish I may
> I wish I might
> Have the wish I wish tonight.

Rhyme, originating in the Balkans, addressed to the planet Venus as Evening Star and patron of happy marriages.

'Would you like some toast, Rose?'

'No thanks. Could I have some of that crunchy cereal – the one with strawberries in it? It's so deliciously unseasonal.'

'Have you tried the shredded wheat with apricots? Soon cereal won't be recognisable as cereal at all.'

'Saga, get down! Leave my crunchies alone! Mary, can't you do something? She listens to you.'

'Come here. Saga! Come to Mummy! There's a good girl! Isn't she sweet?'

'Oh she can be sweet sometimes, I suppose! It beats me why you let the sheep into the kitchen, Mary. You know I'm not an animal lover. I don't even like cats in a kitchen. It's so unhygenic.'

'Sheep are no more or less hygenic than cats, darling! Anyway, Lamia never interrupts your breakfast and, now that Maga's been house-trained . . .'

'OK. Let's not go into that.'

'You are so squeamish. Come here!'

Rose nestled in Mary's arms for a while and then got to her feet. 'I'll do the washing-up and wrap the presents, if you'll do the shopping!'

'Sounds like a more than fair bargain to me!'

Once she had wrapped up all the presents, Rose cut up pieces of leftover wrapping paper and turned them into gift tags. 'To Fiona and Diane,' she wrote; 'Happy Solstice – love Rose and Mary.' She was tempted to put 'Happy Christmas' but knew that Mary would object to this and probably rewrite all the tags.

Mary had some pretty strange ideas, thought Rose, as she put the presents underneath the oak branches – Mary's substitute for a christmas tree. For a start, why couldn't she buy a normal fir tree like everybody else? The decorations were peculiar too: choco-lates, tangerines and nuts, wrapped in red and silver foil. 'I suppose they're cheaper than baubles,' Rose mused, thinking of the tree her mother would by now have installed in her home.

Thick strands of gold and silver tinsel would be wound amongst multicoloured spheres and all those creatures, donkeys, camels, fish – albeit now lacking the odd limb or eye – which she and her sisters had acquired over the years. This year, for the first time, her sisters would have led the rituals and her mother, she was sure, would have been the one to climb the stepladder and place the angel at the top of the tree. The angel was old and every year they talked of getting a new one or even a star to replace it. But her mother said a star was soulless and the new plastic and lycra angels brash and vulgar. So it stayed, the original wooden angel, in its white dress with gold trimming slightly askew and its gauze wings fraying at the tips. Rose would have stayed too – for her mother's sake – just until Christmas Day itself was over, but Mary had insisted, almost distraught, that Rose must stay with her for the whole of the festive season.

She blinked away a tear and looked again at Mary's tree; all red tinsel and holly – at least they were warm colours. Perched at the top of the tallest oak branch was a clay object grey-blue in colour. She had a tiny waist, strong thighs and several breasts – too many in

Rose's opinion. But Mary was very fond of it. She said it was an image of the goddess Diana. Her first love, Flavia, had made it for her during her pottery evening classes. 'Maybe that's why I don't like it,' thought Rose.

She still had one present to wrap – hers to Mary. It seems almost a shame to wrap it, she thought, as she cradled the sturdy cast-iron wok in her arms. She ran her fingers round the rim – so round, so perfect. Mary was going to love this. 'What are you thinking of, my little Rose?'

'Oh – Mary, you startled me. That was close. I've only just wrapped your present.'

'Which one is it?'

'I'm not telling.'

'Well, in that case, let's have some tea. I'm shattered!'

Rose put the kettle on and heard a rumpus at the door. 'Baa . . . baa . . . baa . . . followed by another 'baa . . . baa . . . baa . . .' in a higher register and a different key. There was a scuffling and then a third voice, loud as a trumpet blast, completed the cacophony 'Baa . . . baa . . . baa . . .'

'That must be Lamia,' laughed Mary. She always rolls her 'aas' just like Italians do.'

'It's worse than a Schoenberg symphony,' moaned Rose. 'I don't know how the neighbours put up with it!'

'Well, not everyone thinks as badly of Schoenberg as you do. Doreen from next door positively enjoys it. You should see her staring fondly at them over the garden fence, especially on summer afternoons when she wields her knitting needles out of doors.'

Rose placed two mugs on the table and filled the teapot with lotus flower tea. 'Maybe you should let her fleece them. They'd make beautifully soft sweaters – especially Saga.'

'Rose, how could you? If you had pets of your own, or even children, you could never say such a thing. Come on in, my darlings! Say hallo to Mummykins!'

The moment Mary unbolted the back door, the baa-ing ceased and the three sheep raced towards her, nudging and fighting each other for pride of place on her lap.

'Get away, one of you! I want to drink my tea. Maga – go and visit Aunty Rose!'

'I am not an aunty!' shouted Rose, banging her mug on the table. 'And I don't care if they don't like me!' Or did she? Why did she sometimes feel resentful watching Mary hug the sheep like this? How softly her fingers caressed their fleece, until the wool sprang into tight curls beneath her touch. How warmly, almost passionately, she held them to her breast!

'Surrogate children,' muttered Rose, her voice fortunately submerged by the contented 'baa', uttered by Lamia at that moment. If only Mary would hold her so closely . . . She did, of course, at times, but there was this weird sense of self-discipline. Although they slept in the same bed whenever they visited each other, they were always fundamentally apart. Rose blushed at her own thoughts – but then, after all, they had been going out together for nearly six months. How long was a modern lesbian courtship supposed to last?

Once or twice, when she had drawn Mary towards her in the quiet of the small hours, scarcely aware of what she was doing, Mary had murmured 'Not yet, Rose! We'll be closer when it gets to Christmas. We have to wait for the time to be right.'

'It feels right to me now!'

'Oh Rose, you're so young!'

'Nonsense. I'm twenty-eight, Mary – old enough to know the facts of life, even to have experienced them!'

'I know, Rose. But it's best to wait until we can be sure the Goddess blesses our union. We must wait for the time to be right for her.'

Mention of the Goddess always shut Rose up. She knew better than to argue with Mary over that. If she herself still preferred the concept of being watched over by a benign fatherly figure with a long beard, to a naked clay model with a surplus of breasts, she kept such traitorous sentiments to herself.

'Aa . . . aaa . . . aaaa . . . aaaaah!' sang Mary in the style of an operatic diva as she chopped the vegetables. 'It's Christmas Eve, Rose! Isn't it wonderful? And it's also Friday. It's perfect!'

'I don't get it,' said Rose, attempting to wash the garlic out of her fingernails.

'Didn't you know, Rose, that our ancestors regarded Christmas Eve as more important than Christmas Day? They called it "the Night of the Mother", and much feasting and revellry would be enjoyed that night in honour of the great mother goddess.'

'No, I didn't know,' replied Rose testily, 'But why's Friday so special?'

'Because it belongs to Freya, or Venus, the goddess of love and sexual union. People used to try and arrange for weddings to take place on Friday, so as to gain Freya's blessing.'

'Why should we care about that. I don't know anyone who's getting married today. Do you?'

'Don't you?' replied Mary, looking intensely at Rose over a pile of deftly chopped carrots.

Rose cursed herself for being so obtuse. Tonight must be the night then. Although she had been waiting for this for many months, she suddenly felt nervous.

Rose watched Mary taking out her old casserole dish and preparing to oil it. 'I know. Let's stop cooking for a while and open our presents to each other before the others come. If Christmas Eve is supposed to be our main celebration, it seems the obvious thing.'

'Brilliant idea, Rose! Why didn't I think of it?' Mary responded, grabbing Rose's hand and leading her out of the kitchen.

Mary placed the huge round parcel on her lap.

'This looks amazing – even before it's opened.' She ran her fingers up and down the silver-and-blue striped paper.

'Oh Rose, you shouldn't have! It's wonderful – a mystic cauldron, a cosmic womb, a . . .'

'It's a wok, Mary. I thought you could use it for tonight's meal. That's why I wanted you to open it today.'

Mary gave Rose a hug. 'You're right, Rose – you're a genius! This wok will transform the vegetables into . . .'

'Jordan's Crunchy lasciviously laced with passion fruit? Seriously, Mary, what are we having tonight, apart from vegecereals?'

'Fish, of course, Rose. Friday is fish day!'

'I thought that was a Catholic tradition.'

'The Catholics stole it from the pagans, along with many other rituals, and besides,' continued Mary, her hand playing with Rose's dark wavy hair, 'Fish is a well known aphrodisiac.'

'Mmmm,' murmured Rose.

'Now for your present. See if you can find it!'

Rose looked up and down the tree. Her eyes roamed each branch until they reached the topmost twig with its sprig of holly attached. There was something about it that didn't look quite right. It dawned on Rose that the goddess had vanished. She looked at Mary, who met her gaze with alarm.

'The goddess!' she cried. 'Where is she?'

They looked at the flowerpot to see if it had fallen among the large stones which held the branches in place. Then they scoured the room. Still there was no sign of the clay model.

'Never mind. Let's leave it for now. I want to open my present!' said Rose, secretly relieved at the fall of the goddess.

'Don't be so childish, Rose. We must find the goddess before we do anything else. To ignore her disappearance would be to dishonour Diana.' Mary's voice was harsh. Rose didn't dare to challenge it.

'Just a minute. I have an idea! It's all right, Rose. You carry on looking for your present!'

Rose returned to the tree. From time to time her eyes strayed out of the window. She saw Mary and the three sheep standing beneath the oak tree. Mary was gesticulating wildly, the way she did when she was really angry: though, from this distance, Rose couldn't see the expression on her face.

Saga and Maga – the two smaller sheep – were huddled close together as if fearful of Mary's temper; but the biggest and oldest one, Lamia, stood on her own with her head held high, as if saying she wasn't going to be intimidated. Rose smiled to herself. It would do those sheep good to see their mistress cross with them for once. They got away with too much, they really did. Mary seemed not to mind if they prowled about under the table at meals, bleating and pummelling Rose's legs and feet. They always seemed to butt in during their most interesting conversations and Mary, on occasion, even allowed them into the bedroom.

'Lamia won't do any harm – just sleep beside the radiator to keep warm.'

'Sheep are supposed to live outside. Why do you think they have all that fleece?'

'Oh Rose. You can be so cruel and heartless at times!'

'Don't be ridiculous!'

It's true the sheep didn't do any harm. Rose would sleep, more or less unperturbed. But in the morning she would often wake – at some unnecessarily early hour – and feel rather than see Lamia's head turned in her direction, or Saga's eyes fixed upon her, or Maga's . . .

'I've found her.' Mary burst through the door bearing her trophy aloft. 'Thank God!'

'Thank the goddess!' Rose corrected her facetiously.

'You're right, Rose. Thank you, oh goddess Diana, great Artemis, for vouchsafing to us once again this image of your noble self!'

Rose raised her eyebrows. Diana was reinstated at the top of the tree.

'I taught those sheep a lesson, Rose. They'll think twice before indulging in petty theft again. Maybe I'll let them in the house less often. Have you found your present?'

Rose was already opening the tiny parcel tied with red ribbon, which she had found hidden near the base of the tree. She tore it open. Inside was a little blue box. That could only mean one thing – jewellery. She lifted the lid off the box – and gasped: 'Mary, they're beautiful, exquisite!'

'Try them on, Rose. Let me see!'

Rose placed the earrings on the palm of her hand. The delicate silver stems opened out into beautifully wrought star-shaped frames, each studded with a brilliant turquoise stone at the centre.

'They're lapis, aren't they?' asked Rose, threading the silver stems through her ears.

Mary nodded. 'I found them in Lesbos last summer. You remember the little shop by the harbour in Molivos, where you brought those blue and white bowls?'

'Yes. Oh . . . thank you!' Rose leant forward to kiss Mary on the cheek.

'You're freezing!'

'Am I? Well, it's cold out there you know.'

'Let's go back to the kitchen and get cracking, shall we?'

'Yes. You'll wear the earrings tonight, won't you, love?'

'Of course I will. How can you even ask?'

'Happy solstice, sisters – come in!'

'Hi, Mary. Happy solstice! We've brought some wine.'

'That looks good Ruth. Would you care for a glass of mead while this bottle breathes? Rose, answer the doorbell, would you?'

'You must be Rose – I'm Rachel. It's good to meet you at last. I've heard so much about you!'

'Yes, Mary's often talked of you and Gerry.'

'What lovely earrings! Lapis lazuli, aren't they? They look wonderful with your dark hair.'

'Mary, this fish is delicious!' What's in the sauce? I've never had it before.'

Mary smiled at Rachel. 'It's called lesbian sauce.'

'Oh come on, Mary, be serious!' said Gerry.

'I am being serious, aren't I, Rose?'

'Yes. You see, when we were in Lesbos, we found this taverna by the harbour in Molivos. There was a painting on the wall; a seductive-looking mermaid with long golden hair. She was smiling invitingly at passersby and over her head, in bold black letters, the caption read: TRY MY LESBIAN SAUCE; so we did.'

'Yeah, and it was delicious as you might expect; lemon, garlic, fresh herbs and greek yoghurt all mixed together and slightly warmed. It was the first time,' continued Mary, 'that I ever really understood why fish was considered an aphrodisiac – sacred to Aphrodite.'

'Well,' said Rose, 'It explains why some Catholics still have such large families.'

'I like the vegetables,' added Diane. 'They're sort of crunchy and tender at the same time.' She gave a slow motion munch as if to prove the point.

'We have Rose to thank for that,' said Mary putting an arm around her as she spoke. 'She gave me a wok for Christmas and cutting out so much oil seems to have worked miracles on the vegetables.'

'A toast to Rose!' cried Gerry, 'For keeping us all healthy. May she bloom forever!'

'Pass me the bottle opener,' said Mary. 'To Rose! And now, let's dance!'

'Christ, Mary! After all that food!'

'Oh come on, Pat. It's only once a year!'

Gerry reached out her hand towards Rachel and threw her a pleading glance.

'Oh all right,' said Rachel. 'I'll make a fool of myself if everyone else will too.'

'Hey, look at me everyone!'

'Pat, oh my God, you look hideous!'

'Thanks love. Want a kiss?'

'No, I do not. Take that thing off immediately!'

'I'm going to kiss you anyway! Ruthie, Ruthie, Ruthie . . .'

'*We are family – I've got all my sisters with me!*' chanted Fiona and Diane in unison.

'Slow down, I can't sing and waltz to Sister Sledge at the same time!'

'You just did, honey!'

'Watch it, Fiona. Not so near the tree! Isn't it glorious – all red and sparkling! Shall we dress an oak like that next year?'

'I'm surprised at Mary.'

'Why?'

'Oaks are supposed to be sacred to the goddess Diana. You of all people should know. Harming her sacred grove in any way is supposed to invoke her anger.'

'Does Mary really believe all that stuff? Do you?' Diane drew herself up to her full height and announced with mock solemnity; 'I, Diana, declare myself well pleased with this tree created in my honour. We accept Mary's gifts with pleasure – especially the chocolate ones. Umm – try this – it's praline! Who cares anyway about dressing oaks? Undressing folks seems a much better idea to me. Come closer, Fiona . . .'

'Not here, Diane! Are you crazy?'

'No more than usual. You look divine in that mask, honey – better than usual, in fact . . . ouch, that hurt!'

'Come here, Rose! Let me hold you close. It's coming up to midnight.'

'Mary, tonight –?'

'Yes, my love, tonight.'

'The masks were a brilliant idea for presents, Mary. I hardly know who I'm talking to. Is that Diane prancing about in a devil mask?'

'Yes – at least I think so. They're called mystic masks. I couldn't resist them.'

'Why didn't you get one for me then?'

'Because you look so beautiful as you are. I want to look at you. Hold me!'

Against the grain of the dance tape, Rose and Mary swayed slowly back and forth, Rose with her head resting against Mary's shoulder.

'Look, Mary – the sheep!'

Through the dark red haze of smoke, candles and incense, Rose could just make out the shapes of three animals sitting under the tree.

'It can't be, Rose; must be a trick of the light or else you've been taken in by animal masks. I locked all the doors!'

'Hey Mary!' shouted Pat across the room. 'This is a sheepish trick to play on your friends! You have them well trained, though, I must say. Come on, sheepy-shanks; let's go for it!'

Pat and Maga whirled around the floor in a mad dance. Ruth stood astounded by the mantelpiece. Gerry seized Saga and the two embarked on a passable imitation of a samba. Diane pulled Lamia to her feet and the two careered around the room, charging into half-bottles of wine, knocking over ashtrays, cans of lager, and sending scraps of wrapping paper flying like kites into the air.

'Long live the lambada!' screamed Fiona, in hysterics at her lover's antics.

Each couple, some human, others half-human tried to outdo the others and for a while everything in the room was a wild motion. Rose and Mary continued to sway beneath the tree which was engaged in a dance of its own, red tinsel flapping in time to the stamping of feet on the carpet.

'This is great, Mary, we are having a ball!' called Fiona as she brushed past the tree with Diane once more in tow.'

'A ball, honey? This is more like an orgy. Come on, Fi, let's get closer to the spirit!'

'Rose you look stunning!' Gerry too had deserted her sheepish partner and was breathing deeply. She took off her fox mask and wiped the sweat from her forehead. Let's have a whirl – if Mary allows it, of course!'

Rose stepped forward, laughing, until she felt a restraining hand on her shoulder.

'Sorry, Gerry, I don't allow it. Rose must be mine alone tonight!'

Gerry turned surprised, if slightly glazed, eyes upon Mary. 'You possessive old bag, you. Come on, Rachel, let's boogie!'

Rose looked up at Mary and beyond her at the tree. The goddess was still perched on the topmost branch. Curiously, even though the branches were askew and looked on the verge of collapse, the multi-breasted figure looked cool and unshaken. Eyes like blue flames seemed to bore into Rose's soul.

'It's weird, Mary, look! The goddess is staring straight at us. I never even noticed she had eyes before. What are they made of – some sort of blue marble?'

'I'm not sure, Rose, but I see what you mean. Don't look so frightened. She's beaming approval at you – at us, Rose. That's why you look so wonderful tonight. Venus is smiling upon you.'

Rose looked up at the clay figure again. 'Why does she have to have so many breasts, Mary?

Mary laughed. 'Don't be so prudish! The goddess has a special affinity with animals. Her breasts are to feed and nourish all the creatures of the world!'

'I'm exhausted, Mary, can we go to bed?'

'Yes, love. Let's go. Fiona and Diane can let themselves out. Goodnight, you guys,' she called out hoarsely, 'We're going to crash.'

Somnambulant goodbyes and thank-yous followed Mary and Rose up the stairs.

And that night – what was left of it – they were not divided.

Mary stretched, yawned and stretched again. She lifted her head from the pillow and let it fall immediately. It seemed to have doubled in weight. She closed her eyes. It had been some party – the wildest ever! A mistake, perhaps, to have brought out the brandy after the mead, wine, beer and lager. Ugh, she'd give anything for something milky to take away the dryness in her throat.

'Rose, are you awake?'

Silence. Mary looked blearily towards the other side of the bed. Memories of the night returned; beautiful and sensuous despite the fact both of them had been exhausted. Rose must be up already. She would go down and join her – fix some cereal. This year, surely, there was no cause for alarm.

As she staggered to the bathroom, she tried to brush aside recollections of past Christmases. Flavia, her first love, had brought it upon herself. Those books of esoteric knowledge, the pottery model of the goddess, her attempts to turn the solstice festival into a witches' sabbat; all of that would have contributed. Something, at any rate, had backfired, that first Christmas in Croydon, just after she'd bought the house. It had felt too big for one person and a sheep, but then she had intended it to be for two . . . persons. And, she, Mary, had bent over backwards to try and undo the spell. That's when she had begun to seep herself in mythology and read all those books of Flavia's she had previously scorned: *Astrology, Karma and Transformation, The Cosmic Womb, Druidism and the Celts* and the like. They hadn't been her cup of tea at all. And perhaps her natural antipathy towards her reading matter had shown despite her efforts; for a couple of years later, just when she had accustomed herself to the transformation of her vivacious Italian lover, the same mishap had occurred to Sara.

Mary shook her head as if to brush the memory away. She poured some Jordan's Crunchy with strawberries into a bowl. No sign of Rose. After that – the thing with Sara – she'd thought twice about taking another lover, especially as Flavia hadn't taken to Sara at all. But then, the following year, Maggie had virtually thrown herself at Mary's feet. The more Mary repulsed her, the more Maggie pursued her, until Mary couldn't fight against it any longer. She wasn't in love with Maggie and had intended it to be just a fling. After all, she was a lusty Taurean and she couldn't subdue the sensual side of her nature forever just because of – freakish events.

Damn, she had opened the milk carton the wrong way! Milk was spilling all over the place. She sat down for a moment. After all, she had made the best of the situation. All three sheep were devoted to her, as if they remembered the erotic bonds which had once existed between themselves and their mistress. And they were, on the whole, much more compliant than they had been in their previous incarnation. Rivulets of milk were streaming to the edge of the table and splattering on the lino.

Finally, the truth had dawned. As a Taurean, Mary knew that Venus was her planetary ruler and Venus, therefore, would save the day. If she selected a lover, worthy and beautiful in every sense, and if she genuinely embraced the Venusian goddess as her deity, these base transformations would surely cease. It was her sceptisicm that was to blame. She had always been a matter of fact and practical person, but she would have no more of it! Her mockery of the supernatural and the mystical, her dismissal of ancient legends as gobbledegook had led to her being mocked by these same powers. Now she was a convert. Ignoring her friends' wry glances, she had become a devotee of Diana, a worshipper of Artemis and a servant of Venus, to whom she had shown her intended lover. For Rose, whom she had first spotted at a Valentine's Day disco, had been specially selected as a woman destined to win the admiration of any goddess of love and sexual union worth her salt. The earrings, of course, had been the finishing touch, for lapis lazuli had been prized by the ancient Egyptians for its power to cause rebirth and the 'blue heaven stone' had often been worn in the form of amulets.

Mary finished her bowl of cereal. The spilt milk had finally stopped streaming and the residue lay in a sad puddle on the table. She couldn't be bothered to clear it up now.

'Baa . . . baa . . .!' Oh no, she had forgotten the sheep. They would have been in the house all night and caused one hell of a mess. 'Baa . . . baa . . . baa!' That was Lamia's voice coming from the direction of the sitting room. She had better let them out. She flung open the door and saw that the Solstice tree was still upright – just about. Beneath it, amongst a chaos of wrapping paper, red and silver foil, knelt Saga and Maga. Lamia was crouching beside a pile of tangerines, chocolates and fruit, which had been arranged in a circle, like an edible wreath. In the centre of this wreath sat a tiny black lamb. Its eyes were closed but the rise and fall of its chest proclaimed it alive and breathing regularly.

Tears welled up in Mary's eyes and spilled down her cheeks. 'Oh Rose!' she whispered, as she knelt down in the centre of the circle and picked up the lamb. 'My little Rose – with your dark curls – the most perfect of them all!' She rocked the lamb back and forth in her arms, cradling it like a baby. And the three sheep crept closer and turned eyes of wonder and delight upon the newborn child and its mother, Mary.

The Birds of San Blas

Glyn Brown

Jesucristo, mierda, fuck.

The neon razzle of the Gran Via skids by us, hurtles away out of my line of vision like psychedelic tears down the side of my face. The lights are red at Callao and traffic cop in funky leathers, holster heavy on one thigh like an out-of-whack dick, wades in front of us. Underneath his cap; the hair on the guy is a tragedy. His ref's whistle's bulging out the side of his Brandoesque gob, he tightens his embouchure – very Coltrane, now, very Gerry Mulligan – and fills it with air, blowing like an express. Too bad, my man. As he sees me coming his eyes begin to bulge, he cannot believe the vision and he falls away to our side, arms flailing feebly as flippers. We cruise past in the outside lane, knocking ten or fifteen pedestrians back on their heels, and make speedy work down to San Bernardo.

Just one minute. That leads home, past the maze of warrens round Dos de Mayo, but we can't go there, sweet amiga, it's always lousy with cops. I don't know where I'm headed, and if I took things seriously I'd be in shock, but my brain is lazing, the hundreds of horses between my legs ease to a canter, confused, and the engine ticks over on a turn. I gaze moronically at a cinema hoarding, Madonna cramming her face full of Willem Dafoe. Attack of the fifty-foot woman. She isn't real. Perfect.

'Fred, I can't hold on. Your jacket. Too slippy.' From behind me, somewhere over my shoulder, her voice floats and descends, tiny in the breeze of our acceleration. And this is a femme with a formidable vocal register, grin wide as a pillar-box to let it out of, lips generous enough to snap gum and crack a fast line in quips contemporaneously, à la Carole Lombard, and always slicked vermilion. Laura's appetite for food was nothing much, but for life it was a gargantuan.

I'll tell you what upsets me. It's that she always wanted us to ride this fast, on an outsize motorbike, in a convertible. We used to sit home and watch videos of *Fool For Love* about a million times – she thinks I look like Sam Shepard, I don't, not enough – and she got off like crazy on the opening tune. Which featured some dame baying, 'Come on, baby, lets ride.' Hokey but romantic, Shepard's no fool. (If I wasn't a hood, I'd like to write and direct movies, then be their star. But the nearest I'll get to that is having the right hairstyle.) The song had pretty words, something about 'Ride on into that sad, starry night.' And now we're doing it, and she's too enervated, too dislocated to know. Her hands, slipping from around me.

'Hang *on*.' Those hands, and how they've felt at my waist, their customary place, for the five years since I was fifteen, when we left school. Loosening, now, like a belt you wear every day till it can't hold up your kecks. I get tense, bellow: 'Laura, I'm telling you! Wake up, snap out of it, hold on to me.'

Her head's heavy, lolling on my backbone like a doll's. Tell you why that terrifies me? Because for the first time since I knew her, I feel alone. She's a commanding presence, sometimes too commanding. Still, you miss it when it's not there. With my left hand, I try and steer this tank of a Harley some fool left with its keys in the starter, while somehow I knot her arms round my gut, yanking the long fingers into origami. It hurts, I can tell. So I'm going to let her fall?

'Honey . . .'

It's hard: keeping balanced in a cheongsam and gold mules that don't fit. The dressing up is half the fun – come on, all kids love games – but *que frío*! Must be below zero. Head of transcendantal blond ringlets, mascara pricking at my lids with its creepy, crêpy fronds. The wig waltzes over my eyes and I grip it, rip it off, shove it in my pocket. Quiff is totally fucked. Several lengthy nylon hairs remain enmeshed in my stubble. Wipe my nose on the back of a hand, getting snot on the dinky white cotton glove that leaves no fingerprints. My left foot slips on a pedal, *muy peligroso*, but it would be harder to ride without shoes. Shit, shit, shit. This is torture. In a way, this is fun. Still, we could do with a break. Got that Butch Cassidy and the Sundance Kid feeling. We need a cliff, so we can take a dive.

There's never a breeze in the city. Not since we've been here, I don't think, October, November, December. I can't remember a storm, no gales. But there's a wind tonight. Behind my shades my eyes are streaming. And even the shades, I have to take off now. A city lit at night-time as bright as Madrid ought to be a place you can wear shades until dawn. In reality, it don't work that way.

Her hands, loose again. And we racket down the boulevard toward the Plaza de España. The sky's a diabolical red behind the statue of Queen Isabella, and the stone nereids leap stilly in the fountains. It's a beautiful sight, a vision, a *location*, despite the dipsos and smackheads, the hoods and the droids. I feel warm about droids, tonight. The guys they bring on for the crowd scenes, to fill out the picture, the ones with no lines. The ones with hair so matted and ratty it's alive, and whose lives are only ever gonna be shit because they don't comprendo that, to be a star, you need a good coiffure. I see the importance of hair, sometimes.

'Laura. Darlin'. Look.'

No sound, no movement.

'Sweetheart, you're gonna kill me.' The laugh is high-pitched and stupid. 'My hairstyle's all to fuck, and I know how you hate that. Laura, for Christ's sake, wake up. This is the ride of our lives, and we're not photogenic.'

My eyes are streaming.

In a dream, I once saw Fred in fiery red. You can't miss the devil. Those horns, twisting curvaceously. Hooves, cloven. And more – tail with a pornographic fork and saucy flick, demon, almost slanting eyes (like Sam Shepard's, I thought), scarlet rubber vest from Red or Dead. Fred wants to be a movie star, or a famous heist merchant, but I imagined I had his number, and it was 666. I looked up the definition of Satan when we met. Fred, who loves a comic, believes that of the two of us he's the wise-arse. (Lumme!) So I won't tell him I suspected the minute I saw his green sunglasses (Edgar Allan Poe gave *that* game away). I won't say anything about hypocrisy, though according to Dante the devil has three faces. St Augustine wrote that the flesh of the devil is made of condensed air and, if it is pierced, said Milton, out gushes a blood substitute.

He's not a devil, but it wouldn't surprise me if Fred – Fred the undead, Fred the ill-read, Fred the unbeatable in bed (when he's sober) – had blood substitute in his veins. Occasionally, I wonder just what's real and what isn't about him. For Fred, nothing's real unless it's film. Life's a film. That's why he has no sense of fear. Dumb-arse doesn't know he's born.

Fred doesn't think I'm real, either, if he thinks about me at all. Probably because in his view I look like Faye Dunaway (in my platforms and ripped PVC mini, ah, absolutely). It's a liability. I blame the hair.

Is this the Plaza? Jesus, where's he taking us? On Isabella's flipside, as we swing around and around with a doh-se-doh, the ferrous incarnation of Don Quixote, Sancho Panza doggedly bringing up the rear, always stuck pillion.

This ride's taking forever, and the night is cold. I like it, though. I'm almost numb, and I didn't know we had a bike. And we might as well. Heading nowhere else.

'When you go, what do you want to go as?'
   'Myself.'
   'Unadventurous, in a sense.'
   'Well, that's me all over.' Was she grinding her teeth there?
   'Say not so! My shameless, gun-toting Enfield amour.'
   'Why are you talking like that?'
   'Why not? Entertaining dialogue.'
   Reflective: 'Not shameless, no.' Took my hand with a sigh. Dropped regretful kiss on my palm. I wished I had a camera when she was this pretty. Then turned the hand over and bit my knuckles

with pit bull precision, leaving almost indelible teeth marks, enjoying it, apparently.

'Shit! Stop that. Play with my hair.'

'Thought you'd never ask.'

I leaned back, loving it, threw out my chest bullishly. 'I want to go in my lizard-skin jeans. When I get some.'

'Drama queen.'

'On a sunny day.'

'You'll take what you're given.'

'I want you.'

'I want to cut hair.'

'Later. One job at a time.'

'No less creative. Than what you do. A well-coiffed head is a work of art, like any painting or sculpture. Like any film.'

'Lorrie, please. Don't *create*.'

Fred knows I have a job I want to do. *Hairdressing*. He considers it with wonder. He considers it ridiculous, tragic. He considers it unworthy of consideration, unworthy of me and of someone who is his 'woman', the term he prefers. When he hints that my desire is disappointing and rather squalid, he can't understand why I seem hurt, even though the idea is that it is beneath me and I'm worth more. And I want his *help* with this? For now, he endures it. (His basic take on the matter: 'I want to give her what she wants, but only if it's what I want her to have.') One day, he hopes, I'll relinquish this mad notion.

We circle the Plaza while I think. That's something I like to take my time with.

Christ, she's heavy. Now I truly know what deadweight means. How did we get into this situation? (Rhetorical. I'm on the way back from a job in a jeweller's when I turn a corner at Hortaleza, get deafened by a car backfiring, and see my baby caught up in ugly fisticuffs with two policemen, in the course of it dropping armfuls of purloined artefacts – hairdryer, wholesale-size conditioner, even a heat lamp. She's doing well, fighting her corner impressively, as I sprint across, heart exploding like a field of mines – she's cool, you know, she even looks like Faye Dunaway. She's hitting and clawing, and when I get there I punch the first guy right out and kick the other so hard in the face I think I dislocate his eye, it felt that way to me. Mess everywhere. But then I saw her fall.)

'Why did you do it, honey?' Not the moment. Timing being my one weak point. 'Laura, what was you doing, robbing a *peluquería*?' (That's where the guy lost the eye. Outside a beauty parlour.)

Nothing for a minute, just the sound of cars and the roar of drivers bawling me out – '*Gentuzo*!', '*Mierda*!' '*Gamberro*!' – and then, like a beautiful subtext, a mellow refrain that dips below the melody, I hear her nasal chuckle. With me again. Says a thing I don't catch. 'What was that? *Otra vez, cariña.*'

'I just wanted to enter one, light of my life, and break everything inside it, I'm in that mood. Also I needed some equipment.' She lets go of me, torso swinging loose in the slipstream, and yanks at the pink plastic duffel bag on her back. She's waving something, I half turn. Dislodged into the road, a fiesta of red hot hairdressing equipment and, high-kicking in her hand like a silver dancer, a pair of slick, sleek scissors. 'What's those for?'

A couple of *policía*, one fat one thin, blowing their whistles like Laurel and Hardy, loud and then gone, Doppler effect, as we leave them behind.

'New haircut for you. Because tomorrow's Christmas. Your birthday. *Feliz cumpleaños*, limb of Satan. *Feliz Navidad*.' Her touch of cockney juices the exotic vowels, and she reaches over to stroke my hand, crazy bitch, almost spinning us on our arses. There's a paint streak of blood where she touched me. That's probably the hand that scratched her cop down the chops. The gentleman certainly hit back. Black eye like an oil slick, lips swollen out to here, jutting like Kim Basinger's now. Which she brushes against my neck. 'Rockabilly's dated, even for Madrid. You have to lose those locks.' She clears her smoker's throat. 'Let's go home. It's worse than Smithfield back here.'

'Laura?'
I think she's laughing.

Why? You're asking why I did that *stoopid* thing?

Because you think lady delinquents are beyond sexy, and I let that affect me. Because I'm mad for you, sweetheart. Because the very smell of a rebel makes me weak and I want to dive inside those pants, see what's cookin'. I'm a hunka hunka burnin' love. You're all I need to get by. I'd rather be with him in his world than be without him in mine. Yodelay hee hoo.

That what you want to hear? That's how it was, once. I was putty in your calloused hands. But now I have a dream, and it's not being a second-rate Ma Baker, and it's not even being your personal hairstylist. *Sabes*? You dig?

I think I could drop dead and, despite your words of love, you'd hardly know. I'm wasted. But now I've got my scissors and after I cut your hair tonight, with a flourish, like Delilah, you'll no longer look the part, and for you the look is everything. That will be the end of our adventure. For me, it will be a beginning.

Such speed. Superman, a plane, a bird. I fly her through Madrid, our stolen city.

De Madrid al cielo, they say – after this, only heaven's good enough. And I believe them. The light puts an unexpected complexion on life, illuminates far further horizons. And what else were we to do? Where would've been a better place to go? No one knows us here; we know no one.

I met him at school, back in darkest, most savage Hackney, and I felt a violent attraction the moment he pulled a flick-knife on our RE teacher, Miss Rawkins, name that conjures the notion of peeled, and red she was, as a beetroot, skinny as a carrot. She got a chair, forced him from the room and down the stairs like a rumbustious, bad-tempered tiger. He sauntered backwards, hands in Levi pockets, whistling a happy tune in between puffing on a Silk Cut glued to his lower lip, smiling like an angel. I thought, that hair's divine, needs a trim and a reshape. I offered him a Murray Mint after Geography the next day. He told me he'd thought I was a swot because I sat at the front while he slouched at the back with his feet up, but I sat at the front because I used to be shy, and that was where fewest people could see if you blushed when you answered.

Frederick had a loose, careless walk and bit his nails, and I craved him. We made big plans. Quit in the fifth year for maximum offence, with few career prospects, but it didn't take long. Inside six weeks, I was a hairdresser and he robbed banks, both trainees. We got a hit off what we did, but I cherished the idea of us working together. At the time, I believed this was a recipe for relationship success.

Well, he was a shoddy hairdresser, given the chance. Heavy handed. Too fond of extremes. Forgetful and insensitive, shaving heads unrestrainedly, unwilling to cater to others' desires.

But I could handle his job. It's a terrible thing to do, you know, but I had a knack and somewhere I found a rage to match it. I remembered a man who exposed himself to me in Clapton once, and thought about that. I had been amused, confused, then frightened at the time, and I was still repulsed by men in shiny-arsed brown trousers and greasy donkey jackets, but now I could summon up quite a pitch of fury, and destiny had put dangerous implements in my hands.

My criminal talent revealed itself on our third or fourth raid. Previous to this, I just cut hair while he cleaned out the vault, having lost my position in a lacklustre styling establishment for being too imaginative. I told Fred I had a yen to work on a captive audience.

It operated thus: My lover roped the models to their seats, taping their chops because people talking wrecks my concentration. Then, to the melody of Fred's electric drill, the beatbox playing excerpts from Handel's Water Music, I cut rugs with avant-garde precision and astonishing velocity. Often, Fred was out of my line of vision, but it didn't matter. It may be clichéd but the idea of him and what he was doing, the way he looked when he walked into these buildings and the way his hair curled over his collar made me so excited I felt physically sick.

One balmy evening, the door burst open in a blaze of light and two bellicose gentleman in uniforms hurled their rhomboid bodies at me, bellowing threats and promises. Oh my love! out in the basement strongroom, I thought, deafened by his Black & Decker, ignorant of this.

So I sprayed the foremost of my would-be assailants in the face with an aerosol of curl fixative. He went down in tears, wailing loudly, scrabbling at his skin, mouth twisting like a permed lock. Astounded at my own precocious nastiness, I jabbed my scissors into the second's right hand. Fountains of red gushed out: there are literally thousands of blood vessels in the palm and fingers.

I had hoped to be bad at this; I was not. What helped me achieve such a scary thing was that I have a facility with certain tools and both my victims had particularly ugly hair. One's was a greasy mistral of dandruff. The other's, pale brown, crinkled in a Keegan perm. This should not have affected me, but it did. I was shallower then.

So was my lover; not evil, but an innocent who didn't comprehend the problem. For him it's all flash and celluloid glitter, long shots and close-ups, he sees through a viewfinder, whether or not one is handy. This sounds like the usual lame excuse given for men by women, but Fred has no concept that what he does is antisocial. He lives in a mental CinemaScope, every night a premiere.

I stood about for some considerable time, lulled by the music and the sound of screaming. Fred appeared. He looked at me in a way he never had before. And then he kissed me. His lids closed slowly, waxy and blue-veined as rich cheese, fluttering like the tender wings of hothouse lepidoptera, and he was lost. So was I. I'd sealed my own fate, airtight as Tupperware and far less attractive.

'Sulking? Why did you go along with it, then?'

'I'm a sentimental bitch. I fell for the glamour of nurturing my felonious Romeo. Disgust soon set in, advanced by the tedium of sewing up sartorial rips and tears, soaking blood-boltered jeans and Sta-Prest in biological Daz. I lost interest in your recounting of gory escapades, didn't want to see it, either. And I was jealous. You got better and better at what you do. I'd spoiled you. My temper brewed.'

'I want what's best for you, Lorrie.' (Crunched me to him, five o'clock shadow robber's face stretched for the camera, wretched.) 'But it's a tough job, yeah? Holding up banks. Particularly when you're still learning the language. I need your support.'

The wind in the trees. The sky blue as blue over the Puerta del Sol, its fountains and mariachi bands and our lovers' concerto, histrionics, my own little opera. That chin, and the way you comb your hair like John Travolta. *Te amo* deeply, still. *Estoy perdido* – lost, I'm lost. Strands of coarse damp black in my mouth. I fingered their raddled ends.

'I should've cut your hair long ago.'

The bike takes the corner perfectly, considering I'm supernova tense, and we howl along San Bernado until we hit Espiritu Santo, and begin climbing it. Take a main drag out to the squat. Once we get out there, into the overpopulated crack centre of the city, no one's going to blink at the way we look. Above us, the sky clangs and rattles with yuletide explosions. Christmas in paradise, with Bonnie and Clyde.

We travel miles, from the centre to the suburbs of seedy San Blas. A long ride. As we coast up to our bolt-hole, I see Cabrero sitting in the gutter in a filthy donkey jacket and greasy trousers, taking off his shoes. I'm concentrating on getting the bike parked and getting hold of Laura. Once the shoes are shucked, he removes his socks. And then he produces a syringe and shoots himself in the foot. He throws back his head, soaring. I shoulder the door and hoist her up the stairs. Every step killing. These heels. Drops of blood fall and sink into the wooden treads as into blotting paper.

I get her inside – kicking past her arsenal of hair gel and waxes, shampoos and styling mousses – and drop her on the bed. She's tall. Skinny but long. The platforms add weight. Her hair falls backwards, lank and blonde, dark at the roots. She's too much for me, usually. Her wants and her needs. Brainier than she lets on. New scissors in her jacket pocket; but not tonight, Josephine.

She's white as a sheet. *He studied her face.* The whole of the middle of her is scarlet. And there's a small, neat hole in her shirt. That's ridiculous! But I heard a car, backfiring. I stare, and listen to my heart beating with stentorian authority, like it's milked. 'We are in blood so deep . . .' and something and something, said Francesca Annis as Lady Macbeth.

Wads of cotton wool, and hot water. But the shirt's dried to her. She needed a hospital hours ago, when we began our glamorous spin through the city.

Oh my love, my darling, I hunger for your kiss a long, lonely time. Camera pans back, long tracking shot round the room at the pitifully few items it contains, swings 360°, long take on me crouching here – forsaken, puzzled swain, left to carry the action alone in a towering solo performance.

Laura.

I need your love. I need your love.

She's acting, yeah? Does this reel work or doesn't it?

Fred had a philosophy he tailored to what he perceived to be my needs, feeding it to me as if I were a child, which he used to explain what exactly we were doing, and why we were doing it, and why I should work with him. Fred decided badly presented people – mainly those with poor hairstyles, at which he eyed me carelessly, he's quite transparent – polluted the world. People who couldn't see their own potential, and what life could be if opened out, its possibilities. It offended his sensibilities. He didn't like being reminded of all those droids getting places in hairdo school when I had been turned down, he hissed, pacing the floor with a fury that would get him into RADA, and my accompanying him would draw attention to my situation. My ambition had been cruelly thwarted. This is what he said.

I listened to this crap and watched his mouth, the way his

yellow-tipped fingers played about it. I wondered if Mephis-
topheles had lips like those. I was surprised he seemed to need me so
much, and felt obscurely flattered.

Bells chime everywhere, even here in this pernicious precinct. It's
midnight, and it's Christmas, and at twenty-one I've become a
man. Standing in the half-lit room, looking at myself in her mirror.
Face a Jackson Pollock of splattered slap. I rip off the dress, sit on
the bed in my tights and bra and gold mules and only now does it
come to my attention that one's lost its heel. I reach for a birthday
cigarette, having trouble striking the match.

'I love you, Laura.' The sun was streaming in and we were
dipping custard creams in tea and two thousand smackers better off
since dinner time. She gave me a squint.

'You'd say anything.'

'Meaning?'

She nibbled round the edge of her biscuit in neat, concentric
circles until it disappeared up its own arse. Swallowed tea then
thrust her tongue, a fat wet mouse, deep in my ear.

'It means how do I know that wasn't a fake, wasn't counterfeit?'

'Nothing's real.' I closed my eyes and shivered, thinking of her
tongue, which was disproving my argument superlatively. But I
believed what I was saying. And I said, 'Nothing's anything.' (She
took her mouth away, sighed, 'Oh come *on*.') I continued. 'It's what
you want it to be, and what you decide at the time. Like fake notes,
that's all. If I believe I love you, it's love. Likewise, if you believe
what I say. You receive whatever you believe.'

Even to me it sounded glib. As some sort of proof I said, 'Laura,
let me tie you up,' and she agreed to this. I'm good at it. I thought
that – what we did then – was real, and even now I'm not sure it
wasn't.

We had a replica gun. I told him it had gone to his head.

'Blam. Don't make me laugh. Anyway, it's the picture of you
holding it, you'd look insane.' (Insane, his current word for
wonderful.) 'Pose for me.'

Outside the window, there are pigeons. He shifts his gaze to stare at them. He could do anything. I mean, he's unpredictable, fluid as quicksilver, not open to rational discussion. And, staring at him, I think about something Arthur Miller wrote of his life with Marilyn. 'One could easily go mad shuffling about in this darkness, looking for something real. But the real comes like a bird lighting on a branch after a very long and wayward flight, not reasoned down out of the air.'

Oh my darlin', oh my darlin', oh my *darlin'* Clementine, you are lost and gone forever – whistle through my teeth while I throw clothes about, looking for the right ones – dreadful sorry, Clementine.

On the bed, she's so still I can't stand it.

My profile in the mirror looks insane.

You can't be a hairdresser when you're a wanted woman. They make it very difficult. I'd hoped to create dazzling, baroque displays; instead, my career languished, neutralised, like a bad perm, before it even took. Hating his lazy dismissal of my needs, I stopped coming when we fucked. The give and take had gone between us, if it was ever there. My refusal to take pleasure from him automatically denied his ability to give it. We had no currency in common.

We stayed elusive. He appeared in the papers more than once, though he was small-time. That's as much razzle as there was. I hoped my part in things would be clear. Meanwhile, for Fred the job was nothing less than art, every heist a set piece, and he spoke increasingly fantastic shit. He'd get up whistling, flapping cheerily around our squalid room and often dressing in elaborate suits for work, having promoted himself within his firm. The whistling drove me crazy. He was happy in all this mire.

Laura. Come back.

In north-east Madrid, out past Pueblo Nuevo, you'll find a suburb called San Blas, not wholly unlike parts of London's

Hackney. Here lies the city's biggest prison, and its biggest cemetery, too. Broken houses lean over blasted tarmac filled with puddles, and in the *cervecerías* men lean over festering, stinking messes of offal and guts. The very air in the street smells of meat and fat. If you don't deal drugs, there's little career prospect in San Blas.

But, up above, tied to rusty balconies, there are cages. Canaries, budgies, finches live there. And all day, far higher than the racket of abuse in the *calles*, the bird sing. They sing and they sing, these birds, enraptured, joyous, until they die. As if they could be anywhere, go anywhere, do anything, as if they were in paradise.

No one really sees them, or thinks about them. And if they did, they'd never understand it. Idiots birds. Crazy, trapped loons.

Seven a.m., the Retiro Park on Christmas Day, and the view is sublime. We're sitting, Laura and me, on this resplendent Harley, perched on the monument that dominates the grounds, at the top of the steep stone steps that descend into the lake. A surprising number of people have managed to drown here. On either side of us, there is a vast lion, majestic and serene. They frame my queen and I, and I'll drink to that.

There's no one else around. A coot flaps an awkwardly trajectory, wingtips as it takes off just grazing the halo where the sun mists the water's surface.

We sit for a while, feeling the moment stretch forever. And I wonder if the entire escapade, ultimately, was not simply because I wanted us to end up here, this way. If nothing is real, and everything's an act, how do you know it's finished unless you had the closure in mind? Life's not a rehearsal, they say. But how do they know? I suspect it might be. I couldn't get the lizard-skin jeans, couldn't cram Laura into her jumpsuit. Still, we're in our leathers, and we look, funny valentine, photographable. Your hair's brushed the way you like it. Me, I can't survive without my stylist. Didn't you know?

Tied to me with my belt, she seems surprisingly light now. I finish my fifth Mahou, drop the bottle on the steps and watch its thousand pieces leap and glitter. Whisper, 'Time for our Cassidy and Sundance act, kid,' and rev the bike in first. I wish I spoke American for her – the line would be better – but I only speak cockney.

Once I've said my cue, 'Come on, baby. Let's ride,' we're already going so fast, the steps as we fly off them are like liquid. Wide-angle lens. Picture it.

Angel

Marijke Woolsey

As I opened the window the nets billowed like crisp white sails. I slipped behind them and leaned out of the warm room into the cold darkness. I could hear the sea faintly over the tops of the houses as it rushed and crashed on the pebbled beach. I puffed vigorously on my roll-up, sucking in the calming smoke. Peace. I had escaped for just ten minutes on some weak pretext to do with present wrapping. Fled from the noisy children, the obliging in-laws and my husband engrossed in a book while mayhem raged about him.

I leant further out. Across the lawn, a black hedge and a neighbour's lawn I could see into another family's life, see the warmth of the room from its ochre glow. A room full of rich dark colours, mahogany dining table, chairs and cupboard. Plum velvet armchairs like the one my Grandpa used to sit in. This was a solid, reliable town with people to match. A place where adventure and risk were dirty words.

I re-lit my cigarette and puffed some more. I suppressed a giggle. I felt like a kid again, having a crafty fag round the back, behind the wall, out the window. Feeling smart. Feeling misunderstood.

'What are you crying for?' I sat on the edge of the twin bed next to the one where my sister lay, stomach down, clutching the small, blue plastic radio. She wasn't blubbering, just listening to the charts with tears tricking down her smooth cheeks. I traced the stylised flowers that were crocheted together to form the cream bedspread. Louise sang along, 'It'll be cold, cold and lonely without you to hold this Christmas.'

I padded across the smoky-pink carpet, tufts squeezing

pleasurably between my toes. Out of the clean, rectangular window that covered the middle strip of the end wall I gazed at the view. Hills misty grey at the horizon and bright green close up, spotted with cows and sheep. The black spiky trees, fields of mud, rusty coloured and in front of me down the slope, the village, a single street of little cottages with thatched roofs.

'Never mind,' I said, 'I reckon it's gonna snow this Christmas. That'd be great, wouldn't it?'

'What?'

I didn't turn round but I could feel my sister giving me one of her, 'You're an idiot' stares right in the back of my head.

'You're too young. You can't possibly understand.' Louise dismissed me with this and a heavy sigh. The sort of sound only love-sick thirteen year-olds make. What did I know, I was only eleven. I tried again, 'Yeah, but it would be great if it snowed down here though, cos we might get snowed in an' have ta be air lifted ta safety by helicopter.'

'Being stuck here, here in the middle of nowhere for two weeks, two weeks! is bad enough. Two weeks of no Andy, no disco, no movies, no records, no tapes, no staying up late . . .' She trailed off in a long, low groan.

I left the window, took two long strides, sprang in the air and landed flop on my stomach on the bed.

'Debs!' My sister hissed as the bed creaked and springs twanged beneath me. The record had changed and she wasn't crying any more. She sighed again and said 'You're such a kid. What do you know about love?'

I rolled on to to my back, stared at the low, white ceiling and considered this question. I thought I was 'in love', with an angel. Well, with a boy who looked like an angel. He had shoulder length blonde hair, blue eyes with cartoon-long, fair lashes and soft pink lips. And he glowed. He radiated heat. His skin when I slipped my hands under his T-shirt felt like running your hands over a silk hot-water bottle. When the grown-ups weren't looking and we held hands his were always warm, not sweaty or sticky but dry and hot. At first I wasn't sure about being his girlfriend because he wasn't very tall and I thought the others might laugh but I checked in a shop window reflection and if I wore my plimsolls he was about one inch taller. I thought it must be love because he was the only boy I'd kissed properly like they do in soppy films where you have to concentrate or you can't breathe. Thinking about my angel-boy made me feel shivery and hungry.

'Got any chocolate, Lou?' I rolled on to my elbow facing my sister. She was twirling Andy's ring which she wore on a thin silver chain round her neck. It was a gold signet ring with a black stone.

'Mmmm,' she murmured reaching for the door of the bedside cupboard that separated the twin beds. She pulled at the little brass knob until it made a satisfying twanging sound. She slipped the brown, red and gold outer jacket off the Caramac before slicing the gold foil with one sharp nail and snapping the bar in half.

My angel had given me a ring. I wore it on my left hand, the same finger that my mum had her wedding ring on. He'd given me it back in September. It was a silver band with a small silver flower on the front. He'd nicked it especially for me when he was on holiday with his family in France.

Louise nibbled at the flat chocolate, moaning between mouthfuls, 'I'm too old to be packed off to grandparents for holidays. It's not fair. None of my friends are having to spend more than a few days with theirs. Andy's only going away for two days. I shall miss everything!'

The radio twittered on, an endless stream of alternately extremely jolly or extremely doleful records. I had been going to save my next revelation until Christmas Eve but now seemed the right time. 'Guess what I've got?'

'The plague?' Louise quipped. She had lost interest and was spinning Andy's ring again.

'No. I've got a ten pack of Number Six.'

She swung herself up into a sitting position, 'Show me.'

I snaked off the bed, head first, sliding to where my once white canvas satchel with the smiley sew-on badge and magic marker graffiti lay in a corner. It was gratifying to impress my sister, it happened so rarely.

'We could have one now, if you want?' This was daring but not stupidly risky. Our parents had driven into town. Grandpa was asleep in his armchair and Grandma had gone off up the hill to see if 'the dear old lady' who lived up the top and was younger but frailer than her, needed anything doing.

We drew the thick rose-print curtains right back and opened the left hand window as wide as it would go. Still, icy air crept round us as side by side we leant far out of it, in an attempt to stop smoke blowing back into the room. Louise lit the fag and had the first few drags because she was the oldest and always got to do things first. Then it was my turn. I held the smoke in my mouth keeping my lips together for a moment before blowing it out in a slow stream. It seemed to come out for ages as it mixed with my frozen breath. We passed the fag between us. As this activity had made us more equal than usual I felt bold enough to ask, 'How do you know you love Andy?'

'Well,' she said and then thought for a while, puffing on the fag.

As she pondered I listed in my head what made me know that I loved my angel. Because he doesn't tease or hit me like the boys at school do. Because he's older than me and isn't embarrassed to kiss me in front of the others. Because when we're together I don't feel like eating sweets all the time and can say 'No ta,' all casual like. Because when the whole gang's out he's always looking at me and I'm always looking back.

My sister interrupted, 'Because when we're not together my life is empty and I just want to cry all the time.'

'Wow. I guess you must really love him then.' I said taking a final puff on the fag before spitting on the glowing end and hurling it down the slope to the muddy road.

I pinched the roll-up between thumb and forefinger, getting lipstick on them as I took a last drag. I looked up. The sky was a solid blue-black layer, no moon, no stars, just darkness coming right down. The children's shouts came echoing up the stairs, slipping under the door, trying to pull me back inside. I leant further out. It was a modern house with mean little window sills, a thin strip of fragile wood painted white. I thought about edging out, standing on the window ledge to see if somewhere high above me there was an angel.

The cigarette died. I hesitated, should I put the evidence in the bin, hidden under used tissues? I spat on the end just in case and threw the, little butt out across the lawn. It fluttered and whirled before disappearing into the green-black of the grass. I shut the window against the soothing sounds of the sea, rearranged the net curtains and returned to the fray.

Christmas Plants

Malorie Blackman

'And now we come to the part of the show where twelve lucky, *lucky* viewers will find out what Christmas is all about. Ladies and gentlemen, the moment we've all been waiting for – THE AUCTION OF THE CHRISTMAS PLANTS!"

The studio audience erupted into wild cheers and whistles, following the instructions beamed at them from every corner of the TV studio.

'Every year twelve Christmas plants are made. Only twelve. These plants are guaranteed to last throughout the whole of Christmas Day, ensuring that *you* . . .' Here SSSalinger, the host of *What Am I Bid?* jabbed his finger towards the transmitting camera. '. . . Yes you! Have the best Christmas ever. And all at an affordable price! So get to those video phones! Bidding will start in five minutes. Join me, SSSalinger after these messages!'

Janny pointed her remote at the view screen and lowered the volume until it was just about a background hum. She was sitting on the floor, her legs tucked under her, her head inclined to one side as it always was when she watched the screen.

'Mum, Dad, can I have a Christmas plant? Please. *Please.*' Janny begged.

Her dad smiled at her, but slowly shook his head. 'Janny, we can't afford it.'

'But SSSalinger said they were all affordable,' Janny argued.

'He wouldn't say anything else!' Janny's mum said carefully.

'Oh, please.' Janny persisted. 'If you get me one, I'll never ask for anything else ever, *ever* again.'

Janny's mum and dad exchanged a glance.

'I won't! I won't!' Janny was close to tears.

'We can't afford it and that's all there is to it,' Janny's mum said gently.

'I hate you! I hate both of you!' Janny leapt to her feet and screamed. 'You just wait. You just –'

'Don't talk to us like that . . .' Janny's dad frowned.

'It's my mouth. And I'm thirteen, not three. I'll talk to you any way I –'

'It's on again, dear,' said Janny's mum.

Immediately Janny pointed the remote at the view screen.

'Are you all sitting comfortably?' SSSalinger asked. 'Have you got your video phones ready? Then let the fun begin! For the first Christmas plant, we want bids regarding Central. All got that? Bids regarding Central!'

Janny sniffed hard as she glared at the screen with a mixture of frustration and excitement. She sat down in the chair furthest away from her parents.

'And we already have a caller.' SSSalinger enthused. 'What's your name, sir?'

'Kristofer. Kristofer Donne.'

A man with dark brown hair and the lightest eyes Janny had ever seen was now on the screen, the image relayed from his video phone.

'And what will you bid for this year's first Christmas plant?' asked SSSalinger.

Kristofer Donne licked his lips nervously. 'My sister said Commander Lucas at Central was a slimy turd.'

'Oooh!' The studio audience gasped.

'And what's your sister's name?' SSSalinger asked.

'Lonsee. Lonsee Donne. She works for Commander Lucas at Central.' Kristofer was beginning to relax into it now.

'I'm sorry Kristofer, but I did say bids regarding Central, not a specific person at Central.' Kristofer's image vanished from the screen.

SSSalinger's smile was baby oil smooth. 'Right then folks. Bids regarding Central. Can *you* do better . . .? And we have another caller? Hello, my lovely. And what's your name?'

'Merla Smithe. And I'm here to tell you about my friend, June.' Merla Smithe was already in to it. She waved to the audience via her video phone and blew kisses at SSSalinger.

'And what about your friend, Merla?' SSSalinger prompted with sing-song *bonhomie*.

'My friend June said that everyone at Central should have been stifled at birth,' grinned Merla.

A scandalised 'Ahhh!' exploded from the studio audience. One man fainted and fell off his chair.

'Is the Christmas plant mine?' Merla asked eagerly. 'Say yes!'

'Well, I don't know, Merla. It certainly beats Kristofer and the slimy turd,' SSSalinger grinned. 'Stay on the line, Merla. You never know!'

Janny's mum and dad looked at each other, before turning to look at Janny. Janny was so engrossed with what was going on the view screen that she didn't even blink.

'Do we have any advance on Merla's bid?' SSSalinger asked.

Janny got up and walked slowly over to the view screen which made up one wall of the living room. SSSalinger's face dominated the screen, each of his eyes at least as big as Janny's head.

'Janny, what're you doing?' Her dad asked.

'I want a Christmas plant,' Janny said quietly, without turning around.

'And we have another caller. What's your name?' SSSalinger said.

'Allan . . . Allan Malowe. And I've got one for you.' Allan Malowe's face appeared on the view screen. A good-looking face with a square jaw and wearing round, designer glasses.

'If you don't get me a Christmas plant, you'll both be sorry,' Janny continued.

'Janny, if you don't behave yourself, we'll send you to bed,' Janny's mum snapped.

Janny turned to face her parents. 'I know about you two, you know. Don't think I don't, because I do.'

'And just what does that mean?' Janny's dad asked.

Silence.

'Your father asked you a question.'

Janny walked back to her chair, the slightest of smiles playing across her face.

'That's what she said, I promise.' Allan Malowe looked earnest.

'You heard your wife say this?' SSSalinger questioned.

'She said it to our son, Paul. Ask him if you don't believe me.' Beads of sweat trickled down Allan Malowe's temple. 'She said that if Central were to be flattened by a meteor, she would be the first to cheer.'

The studio audience roared. Boos and whistles filled the air.

'Ladies and gentlemen, we have the winner of our first Christmas plant. Ladies and gentlemen, I give you *Allan Malowe*.'

'Bastard!' Janny's dad muttered.

'Shush,' Janny's mum elbowed him in the ribs, nodding anxiously over in Janny's direction.

Janny carried on watching the screen. The audience cheered as Allan Malowe's grin split his face. Only just discernible behind him were two CSPs (Central Security Police) entering his living room. The first winner's face disappeared.

'Are you ready for the bids to begin on our second Christmas plant?'

'YEAH!!' The studio audience screamed back.

'OK! Let's do it! For our second Christmas plant, we're accepting bids regarding Commander Lucas or Commander Yaksato at Central.' SSSalinger said. 'So *you* get on the phone right now. We'll be back with your calls, after these messages.'

The bidding continued well into the night.

'My friend said . . .'

'My sister told me . . .'

'I was listening to my husband talk to some of his friends and he said . . .'

'They said . . .'

Friends turned against friends, families turned against families – and all for the grand prize of a Christmas plant.

Until at last only one Christmas plant was left. And Janny's eyes were stone hard, stone cold.

'I'm going to bed.' Janny stood up. Without looking at her mum and dad, she left the room.

'Thank God for that!' Janny's mum breathed a sigh of relief and slumped down in her chair.

'What are we going to do?' Janny's dad asked.

'Turn that damned thing down for a start.' Janny's mum said, pointing to the screen. A screen that could not be turned off, only down. 'It's getting worse. We must act soon.'

'How can our organisation compete with Central's plants?' Janny's dad began to stride up and down in front of the view screen.

'Does our person inside Central even know what they look like? Do we know how these ones work?' Janny's mum asked.

'Our best information says they're just ordinary cerebral cortex implants,' said Janny's dad. 'So they'll work directly on the dream centre of the brain.'

'Giving images of the perfect Christmases of the twentieth century,' Janny's mum added bitterly. 'Perfect Christmases . . . No Central, no commanders, no CSPs. That's what we need to get back to – all of us. Not just the corrupt few . . .'

'And twelve back-stabbing, treacherous fools . . .' Janny's dad said with disgust.

They both turned to the view screen, contemplating the spectacle which was still going on, albeit in silence.

'Imagine being able to talk with anyone without being afraid that your words will be misconstrued or reported to Central . . .' Janny's dad said wistfully.

'Imagine being able to trust your own family . . .'

'I trust you, darling.'

Janny's mum smiled. 'I know.' Her smile faded. 'But what about Janny?'

'We'll just have to work harder at persuading her that Central is evil. Our time is coming,' said Janny's dad. 'This time next year there will be no more Christmas implants to tempt others into betrayal.'

'That's this time next year. We have to deal with Janny, here and now,' said Janny's mum. 'You know what she's like as well as I do.'

Janny's dad frowned deeply. He'd seen Janny's eyes as she watched SSSalinger. 'She wouldn't betray us. I'm sure of it . . .' His voice wavered.

'Sure enough to risk all our plans? Our future? Our lives?' asked Janny's mum. 'You're that sure we can trust her?'

Her husband had no answer.

'SSSalinger! Do I win the Christmas plant? Do I? *Do I?*'

'You're absolutely certain she said that?' SSSalinger asked.

'That's it! Word for word – honest! She said 'This time next year there'll be no more Christmas implants. No more Central.' So do I win?'

SSSalinger's image grinned back at her from the screen. 'You most certainly do, darling!'

'Let's hear it for the winner of our last Christmas plant, Ella Nash.' SSSalinger's voice rang out.

The cheers and whistles and claps and stomps of the audience were deafening. Ella turned to look at her husband. He turned away, unable to meet her gaze. Ella turned back to the screen, forcing the corners of her lips upwards to convert her tears to tears of joy.

'SSSalinger, I'd like my daughter Janny to get the Christmas plant, before the CSP take her away from us.' Ella said. 'I want her to understand . . . understand what Christmas was all about.'

But already the CSP were coming through the front door.

The New Year Boy

Shena Mackay

Every New Year's morning, when they were children, Monica and her brothers woke to find a present under their pillows, some pretty sweeties or a tiny toy or book. The New Year Boy had visited them in the night while they slept. Monica had believed that the New Year Boy, like Father Christmas, came to everybody's house, and it was not until later that she had realised that he had been conjured up by her Scottish grandmother. She saw him as a cherub or cupid or *putto*, the depiction of the baby New Year in a Victorian illustration or scrapbook; magical and rather mischievous, with his beribboned basket of gifts.

There was nothing from the New Year Boy now, of course, – it would have been alarming if there had – but when Monica woke on New Year's Day and groped for her glasses on the bedside table, she encountered her new diary. She held it in her hand, knowing it to be a jaunty little fellow in a red jacket, with a pencil at the ready like a neatly furled umbrella, or perhaps a sharp, slim, cheerful chap in a flat cap. She smelled the newness of the pristine white pages sandwiched between red covers. As she lay in her large bed, under the billowing quilt and embroidered covers, a big woman in red satin pyjamas, she was at the heart of a kaleidoscope; before she put on her glasses the room was a shifting jumble of colours; glitter and clutter, dull gold of icons and gilded *putti* and baby angels who flew about the walls playing musical instruments. Rich dyes and designs of fabric and tapestry glowed in dark jewelled tones.

Sometimes at night, when the old house shifted, a string of a mandolin twanged, a balalaika throbbed a deep note in the darkness, a zither sighed, or the piano started from a doze with a loud crack of contracting wood. Monica taught the piano and the guitar, but she retained her childhood love for the harmonica. It had been love at first sight; the moment she had set eyes on that mouth organ in the music shop window, grinning through wooden teeth set in red tin lips. She had known it was her instrument, for it had her name on it – Harmonica. It could be cheery, it could be melancholy; its merriest jig had undertones of the blues. She could never pass an indigent old busker wheezing out 'Scotland The Brave' without flinging a coin into his cap. Every conceivable joke about her name had been made long ago.

When she opened the heavy curtains the moon still hung like a mistletoe berry in the grey, hungover sky; to the east clouds were cold dirty cinders with flashes of unburnt silver foil and orange peel. She turned on the radio and came in on a dirgey Stabat Mater droning echoes of chilly stone in clouds of powdery incense. She switched it off, snatched up a harmonica and treated the people in the upstairs flat to a brisk rendition of 'A Guid New Year Tae Yin An' A'', and tidied up the kitchen while her bath was running.

The New Year had been seen in with a few friends; Monica had served ginger wine and black bun sent from Scotland, cherry brandy and slivovitch in gold-rimmed glasses painted with fruit. On the last stroke of midnight a first-footer had lurched over the threshold. He was asleep on the sofa now. Monica had forgotten all about him, and the mouth organ and the clatter of dishes had failed to wake him. A first-footer should be dark, and this one had a mat, almost a mattress, of grey-white beard and hair, both wiry and soft like hanks of sheeps' wool caught on a fence. Paper chains susurrated gently in the snores that were drowned by the running of the bath taps, broke from their moorings of sellotape on the ceiling and covered him in pastel coils. Peter, twice-divorced, a piano shifter by trade, slept on, sprawled across the inadequate sofa, a huge man in a soft shirt like a Russian peasant's blouse and trousers still tucked into boots. His unconscious was telling him that it was safer to stay asleep because he would not remember if he had carried out his intention to propose to Monica.

*

Monica, who had been a widow for fifteen years, stood spoiled for choice in a bathroom full of scented soaps, talcs and bubbles. She had no children of her own. She was an Aunt. An aunt decreed by her nephews and nieces, and her pupils, she thought, to be the cleanest aunt in Christendom. Old students sent her photographs of their children, and sometimes the children themselves to teach. Several of her pupils had done well: 'taught by Monica Baker' did not have quite the cachet of 'studied with Nadia Boulanger' but there was her name in the potted biographies in the programme notes, and that gave her great pleasure. She had come upon another, twanging out 'The Streets of London', in the underground at Picadilly Circus.

'You can do better than that, Michael,' she had said, and fined him ten pence as was her custom, for sloppy' practice. Monica adored her brothers' children, loved introducing them, saying 'This is my nephew' or 'These are my nieces', presenting them like a bouquet of spring flowers. Her favourite niece had given her the diary and Monica thought of her now as she stepped into fragrant bubbles, her dark hair that smelled so fresh, of sun and wind and faintly of the sea. She wondered if her own hair had had that perfume, when she was young, with her young husband. This morning she would walk in the park, as she did every New Year's Day, and remember him. He had died on the first day of the year, when the scent of hyacinths, so blue and pure and piercing had filled this flat.

As she padded back to the bedroom in her robe to dress, she noticed for the first time how stale and nicotine-smelling the air was. She must open all the windows, especially in the sitting room, and fumigate the place before she went out. She had an engagement that afternoon, playing the piano at a New Year party at a nearby retirement home, although it was a mystery to her why previously some people should exhibit, as a symptom of geriatric decline, a sudden desire to play bingo and sing songs from the Boer War. She would take along a harmonica and try them with a few riffs of Dylan and Donovan. There would be cake and paper cups of sherry. Last year, when pressed to imbibe the dark sweet liquid she had conceded with 'Oh, just a thimbleful, thank you, I insist . . .'

The young Filipino nurse had looked bemused and disappeared, returning ten minutes later with a battered silver thimble, into which she solomnly dribbled three drops of sherry. This year Monica resolved to accept her paper cup with a good grace and leave it undrunk on the top of the tone-deaf piano.

Dressed in magenta and mazarine blue, Monica strode in her green boots into the sitting room, and screamed. Peter jumped to his feet, smacked in the eye by a walking hangover. A black cigarette fell from his lips to the carpet. He ground it out with his boot. Monica stamped her foot in its green boot. He watched with dull interest; he had never seen anybody stamp her foot in rage before. Had he or hadn't he asked her to be his wife? He thought she might be a bit – colourful – to face first thing every morning. Her eyes were framed in harlequin rims.

'You're looking very – bright,' he said. 'Oh, I almost forgot, I brought you something last night. A New Year present, but I didn't get round to giving it to you.' He fished in the pocket of his army-surplus greatcoat which was slumped in a corner, and pulled out an empty vodka bottle. He dropped it and it rolled away, a glass cossack hopelessly drunk on parade. He drew something from another pocket.

'Happy New Year.'

It was a broken hyacinth in a pot.

Monica snatched it, rushed over to the window, and flung it out. 'I'm going for a walk!'

Pausing only to slash a scarlet lipstick across her mouth, throw on a necklace of heavy amber and a viridian poncho, she dashed out of the front door. Peter lumbered after her, struggling into his coat.

'Something I said?' he panted. 'The hyacinth? I'll get you another . . .'

A drizzling rain was making the park very green. Monica stalked in tears past the bench in the bare pergola where she had intended to sit holding the hand of her husband's ghost. Peter pounded along beside her.

'Monica, wait! About last night, did I . . .?'

'Go away. Please. I need to be alone with my thoughts, I – I've got a professional engagement this afternoon.'

'A gig?'

'An engagement. I don't play gigs. I'm an artiste.'

Thirty years ago she had played a summer season at the Gaiety Theatre, Ayr, billed as the Nairn Nightingale, accompanying herself on the concertina, with the Jinty McShane Dancers, game old birds in tartan tutus, pirouetting behind her. A squirrel watched them from a branch, now.

'I'm sorry, I've nothing for you,' said Monica.

She remembered the warm gingerbread boys with melting icing buttons that she had made for her pupils.

As she spoke, an old black bicycle wobbled round the corner, a small boy at the pedals, and a panting father clutching the saddle from behind to steady him. They careened to an ungainly halt.

'Excuse me,' Peter said. He unwound the long scarf from the astonished and perspiring, but too puffed-out to resist, father's neck and looped it round the boy's waist, putting the two ends in the father's hands.

'Try it like this,' he said. 'It never fails.'

They got the bike upright and Peter muttered in the father's ear, 'The trick is knowing when to let go.'

As father, bicycle and boy riding high and confident disappeared into a green blur Monica had to wipe her glasses, both sides of the lenses, and as she replaced them she saw Peter's terrible mat of hair and beard spangled with silver drizzle, and perceived him in that second as a viable proposition. Perhaps . . . she visualised a pair of shears – there was enough of it to stuff a cushion – and remembered an electric razor of her husband's that she had kept, an obsolete old Remington with twin heads of meshed steel.

Peter, meanwhile, had found an irritating bit of walnut shell stuck in a tooth, and recalled that her books were double-parked on her shelves. There would be no room for his own.

'Peter . . .'

He looked at her; a tough nut to crack, an obdurate Brazil, a tightly closed pistachio. He had had a narrow escape.

'I'll leave you to your thoughts,' he said, and left her on the path.

Later, at home that evening, regretting the cup of sherry to which she had succumbed at the elderly residents' party, Monica thought about the electric razor. Suppose she had taken it from its case and blown away a speck of hair, a tiny particle of him which she had; lost for ever. The old-fashioned radiator rumbled, the wind whimpered in the chimney, and a drift of soot pattered the paper fan in the fireplace. She settled comfortably, a magpie in a big glittery nest, with room to stretch her wings. She reached for her diary and began entering her name and address with faint anticipation. All those white pages, waiting to be filled.

The Christmas Cactus

Maude Casey

At some point during the early stages of the Cold War, Anna's parents had bought another bath. They had no room to put it in, so they kept it under the stairs. This took some manoeuvering, as well as the removal of five or six pieces of tongue-and-groove which boxed in the whole of the area under the banisters. Her mother yelled, her father roared, the baby screamed, and pieces of dull wood splintered beneath the chisel. Her father's nose had a drip on the end of it, and the piece of hair which he usually wore brilliantined back over his head, hung lank and demented in front of his face. 'You and yer flamin' stupid ideas,' shouted her mother, as the bath locked rigidly into place across the full width of the hallway. 'Lift up yer bloody legs will ya,' she continued, slapping and prodding her children's shoulders, as they climbed first into, and then out of, the bath on their way to school.

Now that Anna is a woman and has children of her own, she knows how easy it is to slide into a whirling gulf of hysteria when faced with the dumb, intractable sabotage inflicted by objects in the material world. Especially in the mornings, when, frog-marched by imperatives, she is getting the older ones ready for school whilst also feeding the smaller ones. Before 8.30 on any weekday morning, Anna has grappled with perhaps 100 inconveniences. These include drawers that won't open more than three inches, a grill pan whose right handle is held on by a flimsy piece of fuse wire, a high-chair whose back rungs are exactly the right width apart to trap a baby's foot at a dislocating angle, and three lunch boxes, each with its unique foible. She does these things in a kitchen where she and her children have to walk sideways and eat standing up. She gathers and fixes and does up: buttons, shoelaces, pony-tail bands; zips, harnesses, swimming gear and books. If the children are late, they will get detention, and it will be all her fault. She tries hard not to dislocate the smaller ones' limbs as she inserts them into garments, and is surprised at how often she succeeds, considering.

The idea of the bath was not her father's anyway. It came from a small, buff-coloured booklet he'd been given, entitled *How to Prepare for Nuclear Attack*. The bath was to put things in against fall-out. Anna has a confused wisp of remembrance, of an eau-de-Nil tub full of milk, pale in the moonlight, and of giant cans of spam and corned beef. In true life, the bath was filled with water, to preserve a fresh supply for drinking. Her father covered it with a large piece of carpet felt. The squat, hairy, dun-coloured shape looked like some ponderous sleeping animal, breathing silently but remorselessly. Anna crept past it holding her breath, so as not to waken it.

Having safely delivered her older children to their schools, Anna returns home with the two younger ones. Her progress is slow, since she has one baby in a buggy and another by the hand. Or, if she's lucky, by the hand. Mostly, it's a matter of coaxing and steering a staggering little bundle of erratic and unpredictable impulses, through a minefield of traffic, kerbstones, dog mess, vomit and broken glass. This is peacetime, thinks Anna, this is not Bosnia, as she prevents the little hands from triggering apocalypse. There are no snipers on the rooftops, no tanks on the cracked pavements, no road-blocks at the end of her street, and eventually she reaches home safely with her children. She is relieved that, especially at moments of crisis, such as crossing roads or passing sweet shops, she has somehow managed to generate patience and generosity; to say, look at the trees, at the pigeons, look at the big yellow truck and the fat white clouds. In fact, apart from squeezing the older one's hand just a touch too tightly, she has not laid a finger on either of her children. Nor has she clawed out the eyes of any motorist or hurled bricks though estate agents' windows, or run amok through the glaring, brazen Christmas displays in the toy shop.

When she opens her front door, it jams against a heap of junk mail. Christmas bargains shout at her from Toys R Us, from Boots, from the DIY stores, and offers to lend her thousands of pounds clamour from a host of shrieking envelopes. Her older baby toddles in crowing and chirruping over the brightly coloured fistful of cars and dollies and war toys she clutches in her hand, and Anna drops the remainder in the bin. Her forehead is furrowed with the effort to remember what it is that you retrieve from all the garbage in order to make Christmas for your kids. What is it that you'd like them to feel, and to remember when they're older, from all the heaps of greed and fear and anxiety? What myth of perfection can you hold in your arms and say, ah yes, *this* is real, this matters? For now, she is pleased that she has not wasted her energy on useless rage in the streets outside, for the day has barely begun, and she knows that her reserves of calm unselfishness have yet to be plundered to their depths.

What does she do, all day? How many things *can* a woman with small children do in one day, and all at the same time? Picking up and sorting, wiping, scraping, sweeping; assembling food and preparing it, having it spat at you and wiped in your hair; cleaning noses, bottoms and hands; knowing at all times where you can find scissors, sellotape, glue, and how many variations there are of six toilet roll tubes, a cornflakes pack and flour and water paste; knowing which pillow the tooth fairy will visit tonight; making everything come out all right or very nearly. In such a busy life, Anna doesn't quite know how she is going to find time to make Christmas, all the stockings, all the food, the tree, the hope and wonder, the benevolent spirits who visit children on one night of the year. At such times Anna feels that the top half of her brain is missing, and that other parts of her have become quite hollow.

The bath was something to do with the Bay of Pigs. Its coarse bristles brushed her legs as she leaned across it to take a can of peaches from the shelf under the stairs for her mother. She imagined it scampering across a shingle beach, its trotters scattering stones, making tiny avalanches down to the sea, the grinning tusks curving slyly like the sickle moon as small black eyes glinted with wickedness. Overhead, a plane droned across the sky, and she stood holding the tin tightly to her stiff chest, until the winged snout had drilled its way over the street, over the house and beyond. So far, so good, she whispered, as she ran into the kitchen.

In the early afternoon, if both of the children are asleep at the same time, Anna sometimes has a whole hour to herself. Today, things are going well so far. The older one is sleeping, her breath barely stirring the downy curls around her face. Anna is sitting comfortably in a low chair, with the baby lying across her body, sucking strongly. Before he began feeding, his whole being was a scarlet, fisted scream, blotched with livid purple. Now, his skin is suffused with pale rose, all silk and alabaster. Sometimes he splutters as the milk gushes too fast. It always takes a few months after the birth of a baby for Anna's breasts to settle down, to stop engorging and spurting. If she is naked, thin blue threads of milk will sometimes arc across the room and hit the window or the potted palm, like the birth of the Milky Way, or was it Venus? She feels that this is the closest she will ever get to knowing what it's like to have a penis, this involuntary swelling and springing into action, followed by streams of milky fluid. She wonders what would be the closest a man could get to knowing what it's like to give yourself to someone smaller and weaker, day in, day out. Musing thus, Anna stretches her legs and flexes her toes. She likes to feel the muscles of her thighs harden as she clenches them. The baby too likes to involve his whole body in the business of feeding. His hand in particular is never still. All five fingers spread, he feels the air on his skin, holds his hand a millimetre away from her breast, prolonging the moment of contact. A soft pat, then a hard little fist, then a swipe at her hair, yanking it down. And then he punches her cheek, pauses, clutches her shirt, feeling for texture with his thumb while his index finger thoughtfully flicks the edge of a button. A fist again, held against his own cheek now, moves up his head, extending a finger to feel the wispy filaments of hair. He squeezes thumb and finger together so that they resemble perfectly one of those birds on top of totem poles, all eyeless, fat curved beak – and snatches at his hair, pulling, wrenching, his whole body twisting against hers, as one waving foot dabs her lips and he grabs his ear with his whole fat hand, jerking it down, a sudden scarlet lever. The rounded, never-walked-upon heel is against her mouth, the five berry toes search her lips. All of this takes about half a minute, but it has also somehow expanded to fill the entire universe of space and time and tilting worlds.

After she'd given her mother the can of peaches, Anna had stood against the draining board, with panic hacking at her throat and scrabbling with red-hot needles at her skull. The plane had left London, but it was droning its way westwards, over Wales, over Ireland, to where she stood every summer holidays with her uncle leaning on the gate, watching the cows move slowly over the back meadow to the milking shed with their udders swaying between their legs. If the bomb did drop, you'd have to milk them, only then you'd have to pour the milk away. She saw glossy rivers of white, mirroring the faint blue of the morning sky, flushing dung from the yard and swirling down the gutters. And the cows would move through the beautiful, silent morning grass, through swooshes of lethal dew, their udders stuttering with fallout, the geiger counter clickety clicking in the hedgerows. From then on, this picture was in her mind every day at school, as the nuns had the whole class kneeling on the thick wooden floors. Heads bowed over rosary beads, all classes suspended for days, they prayed that President Kennedy would somehow be reached by the angels of wisdom and peace winging their way to him from this North London school, by way of his Irish roots.

The baby's eyelashes curl up from his cheek. He is all arabesques. He pats his plump warm thigh with an open hand, grabs his toes and straightens his leg. Rhythmically, with his hand he draws his leg outward and back, outward and back. He is widening the perimeters of his world. She folds his thigh in her hand, feeling the soft baby flesh, hard as nails beneath the satin skin, exactly shaped to fit the palm of her hand. His clear dark eye, gazing imperatively into hers, reminds her of the heart-stoppping zone of ecstasy she swam into each time she held a baby she'd just delivered in her arms and met those cloudless eyes for the first time. She feels she is turning into pure essence, and then he burps and splutters. This is where we come from, she marvels, and where now shall we go?

At some point during the later stages of the Vietnam War, the phrase 'carpet-bombing' evoked that bathtub all over again. Anna saw then, in her mind's eye, lumbering B52s unfurl sinister, bristling swathes over rivers, plains and mountains. She saw villages and fields with people in them working, heard the lazy meandering drone as people looked up, one arm shielding the eyes from the sun. She saw lost cattle stumbling through smog over blistered land as mothers ran and ran with their children. And at some point during the damp, held-back Spring when Chernobyl washed all green leafy vegetables and the black boughs in the park dripped on her baby daughter, the bathtub stumped into her mind again, as she wondered if the water running from her kitchen tap really was crackling. She kept seeing all the pregnant women of the Eastern block, and all the baby girls whose tiny ovaries already contained the future, fleeing through blockades of overturned churns. She pictured the entire globe covered with people on the move, carrying blankets and cooking pots, each mother cradling a baby inside a fold of her garments.

She transfers her baby to the other breast and curls her shirt protectively around his head. In the Tigris Euphrates valley, the cradle of civilisation, the place where language first bit its way on to clay and stone, war is etched upon the desert floor and rolls in tides from the slow-moving surges of a bloated sea. Swollen by engulfing oil, it plops like treacle around clotted feathers and long necks tatty as dying beaks stretch exhausted to a black sky. As the baby's sucking becomes more drowsy, Anna notices that vagrant, swirling images from television screens are beginning to cluster more thickly round his head. Clouds of smoke hang over Mesopotamia like a shroud. Machine-gun fire pounds in Bethlehem, shredding small brick houses. Thudding phalanxes of Gameboys and Nintendos crawl crab-like round the room, and *Terminator Two* begins to bellow from the skirting board. A baby peeps over the grainy black-and-white shoulder of a perfectly endowed young man who is selling private health insurance. Yacking batteries of baby dollies wee and wail and squirm their rubbery limbs for Mama. So this is Christmas. Anna waits, cradling the baby more closely to her as his weight begins to settle into her body. Lines of women in headscarves and shabby coats shuffle slowly through the room with shopping bags. Among them she slowly recognises her cousin Kate in Belfast standing with her children, waiting for her carrier bag and her baby's nappy to be searched by a group of teenage soldiers whose faces are obliterated by warpaint. Machine-guns are adjusted level with the children's heads. Kate is chatting with her children, an arm round Roisin's shoulders, smiling now and then at the baby. Anna starts to call her, but of course she disappears.

Her baby is asleep now. His lips are falling like a bud from her nipple. He lies like a blowsy peony, in a swoon of milk and sleep, safe inside himself. The boundary between herself and him is beginning to form. Across his countenance, over lips and cheeks and along the lines of his brow, there travels ceaselessly the features of each generation of the families that brought him here. Anna catches a breath of his dear sweet newness as she carefully stands and places him in his cot. All the objects in the room are settling calmly and peacefully in their proper places around the sleeping infant. Anna stretches her arms above her head and walks over to the window. She may have a bath or wash her hair. There is a plant upon the window sill that needs re-potting. The Christmas cactus in its brass bowl is calling her to notice it. She looks and sees that the tips of each of its jointed limbs are turning coral-pink. Flowers are forming. She feels like singing. 'So far, so good,' she whispers.

Ghosts

Caroline Hallett

Molly and I walked hand in gloved hand to the Combined Schools Carol Concert, our ghosts clutched firmly in our free hands. We were in the middle of a long line of children, one of five lines converging from junior schools in the town and outlying villages towards the gloomy candlelit nave of All Saints Church.

From our school we had to cross the green, where the cold, stored in the winter earth, welled up through the muddy paths and entered our feet, passing easily through our polished shoes and clean white socks. The chattering line quietened here and lost its rhythm. Children hesitated, shivered, straggled and were left behind, shrinking into their coats. Two teachers shooed at us from the back.

'Keep moving children! Sally! Pick your feet up! Who's your partner then? Hold hands children, keep in line!'

I stopped to stare at the brimming pond, its surface faultless and bland, but harbouring a depth of cold that I sensed capable of penetrating people and freezing them at their core. I held on to myself and watched the moorhens swimming in smaller and smaller circles. This was surely the coldest time of all, just before a freeze. In the failing light the smooth water was already flecking up with tiny shards of ice. Molly tugged my hand.

'Come on, you'll freeze to death. Have you got hold of him still?'

'Yes.'

'They don't feel the cold you know.'

'I know.'

I felt safer when we left the green and crowded into the dark twitten, heads down, giggling and whispering under the glistening laurels. There was a short stretch of pavement between the twitten and the churchyard. It was here that Molly stopped, suddenly, and shouted at him.

'Off the bloody road, you idiot.' (This she got from her mother.)

The line of children bunched up behind us and someone laughed loudly. It was clear that nobody was in the road.

'Don't worry Molly,' I said 'They can't get run over. Cars just go through them.'

'It's not that, silly,' said Molly 'It's me I'm worried about when I have to run out and grab him. I don't know what's got into him.'

I could see what she meant. Carloads of anxious parents, smart, powdered mothers and stiff-looking fathers were edging past us looking for parking spaces.

I was surprised at Molly's ghost playing up like that. It wasn't like him. Mine was the frisky one, if anything. I was always having to calm him down and talk to him, like I did to Molly, 'Hold on now, slow down!' Sometimes I felt that between the two of them I was losing all control. Molly's was usually quite lazy and needed bucking up. 'Get a move on Jack,' she'd say. This was her nickname for him, not his real name. We didn't know their real names. Ghosts were quite a new thing with us, we were just feeling our way really. Before that we'd had horses which were somehow more predictable.

I thought Jack was probably playing up because of Molly's nerves. They have a sixth sense. She was to sing a solo at the carol service, not a very long one. She said she wasn't nervous, but then I didn't know how she would tell, as she seemed to me to be nervous all the time. She could not sit still.

I became friends with Molly by accident. A lot of things happened to me by accident. She was a new girl in our class and Miss Rawlings asked me to show her round. 'Make her feel at home,' she said, 'Imagine you'd never set foot in the school before and think of all the things you'd need to know.' I didn't know if I could do it right. Molly followed me round all day while I explained portentously, 'These are desks where we write our work. These are tables where we eat our dinners. These are sinks where we wash our hands.'

'And these are toilets where we do our plops,' said Molly. We laughed. I felt a weight lifting. Molly could do this. She didn't brood like me. She had a lightness about her, she could shrug things off.

A lot of the girls didn't like her. They took a while to make up their minds, but once they'd decided, it was uphill for Molly. They were slow-moving small-town girls with tight pigtails and curling lips, their socks startling, their dresses crisp and neat.

'Oh look! It's Molly the new girl.' Their lips curled. 'Hello Smolly! Hello Smelly Smolly!'

Molly came from London and her socks weren't always clean. Her father had taken over as greengrocer when Mr Dingley passed on. The town wasn't welcoming. There were snobs everywhere. Even my own mother wouldn't go near his shop. She said his apples were soft, but I knew that wasn't the only reason. She sighed when she talked of Molly and her big sister Jane.

'Poor things!' she murmured.

All my efforts couldn't persuade her to cross the threshold of Molly's shop. She would rather trek to the farm or wait till market day. 'These farm apples are wormy,' I'd say, spitting chewed up chunks into the rubbish bin. 'Pah! Ugh! Why don't we go to Molly's dad's? He's got russets in now. They're nice and hard and the skins aren't bitter.' My mother would purse her lips together, as though she could already taste the bitterness that I disclaimed.

'Russets are not my favourite apple,' she'd say, 'And besides it's not just his apples. His carrots have seen better days and the spinach looks tired and mangy. I wonder how clean it is in there. Have you noticed his hands?' This was not a question. I thought about Molly's father's hands. They seemed ordinary to me. I wondered whether there was some hidden dirt under the skin, a kind I didn't know about.

'Well you can't blame him really . . .' she went on. 'He's had a lot to cope with, poor man. You don't have to go in there to know that. You can hear her carrying on from way down the street.'

Molly's mother wasn't someone I knew. I'd hardly seen her, even when I played with Molly after school. We walked back from the bus stop and sometimes I'd stay and we'd help her father out, piling wooden trays in the back of the shop, picking out the mouldy grapes and squashing them with our brown shoes, making towers of oranges in blue tissue nests. Occasionally he gave us cherries to eat and we had pip spitting contests, aiming at the other side of the street and hitting the legs of passing shoppers. I never stayed more than half an hour, because I knew my mother would rather I wasn't there at all, although she never said so. Molly's mother never seemed to worry about where she was. She stayed upstairs with the curtains drawn. Molly said her head hurt a lot.

I knew I would be friends with Molly when the girls started calling her Smelly. I felt fiercely for her, although she never seemed bothered herself. She would shrug. 'Smelly yourself, you fat little cow!' She had a few answers up her sleeve, words that we small-town girls hadn't heard before. Her voice could go hard and shrill. I didn't know if I liked her, but I knew somehow that I would defend her, and she, knowing this too, stuck to me.

One playtime in summer, Molly and I crouched in the shade under the bushes at the edge of the playground.

'Let's rub bellies,' she suggested. We knelt down and lifted our skirts. We were hot and our bellies were slightly sticky.

'Let's snog,' I suggested.

'Girls can't,' she said knowingly.

'Why?'

'Girls don't snog girls and boys don't snog boys. That's all!'

'Oh.'

After we'd rubbed bellies Molly said 'I suppose we're best friends.'

'I don't think we are,' I said, 'But we might be one day.'

'Oh we are for sure,' said Molly.

I never felt sure like Molly. About anything.

The teachers loved Molly because she was quick on the uptake and different from the others. The girls picked on her and the teachers picked her. She was chosen often, to hand over flowers on sports day, to lead the chanting of the school creed, and now to sing the solo for our school in the Combined Carol Concert.

As we turned through the wooden gates, under the yews and into the graveyard, I thought Molly seemed more nervous than ever.

'Slow down Molly,' I said, tugging at her sleeve. 'What about the ghosts? Will they go in the church with us?'

'No, course not. Ghosts don't go in churches.'

I didn't question her but she went on. 'They're two different things. They don't mix. Besides they wouldn't behave themselves these two. We'll leave them in the porch. They can play round the gravestones.'

We patted our ghosts in the porch.

'Off you go!' and they flitted off, as far as I could tell.

I sat next to Molly in the choir pews near the altar. She was fiddling with everything in sight, the hassock, the hymn book, her buttons. Then her sock caught in a jagged splinter of wood in the pew, and she worried at the loose thread; twiddling it round and round her finger.

I saw my parents arrive at the back of the church, my mother clutching her bag high up on her chest and craning and darting her head in a searching arc, looking for me. Then she caught sight of me, gave a small wave and jabbed excitedly with her gloved finger, prodding my father who smiled uncertainly into the gloom. They seemed a long way off.

The vicar floated up the aisle, like a duck on the canal, gathering choir leaders on the way. The muffled drone of greetings died away. Everything was ready to start.

'Aren't your parents coming?' I whispered to Molly.

'They should be.' She craned past me to squint into the distance, then settled back to pick at her sock. The vicar stood to welcome parents and friends from five schools to this popular annual event. His voice was strangely reassuring, like the soughing of wind in the pines. I relaxed into my seat and stared at the dusty creche by the pulpit. Finally he stopped and sat down.

In the absolute quiet before the first song, even before the choir leaders lifted their hands to signal the drawing in of hundreds of breaths, there was a flurry at the back of the church. The wide door squeaked open and a couple made a noisy entrance, the man supporting the woman, who swayed towards the pews. Heads turned and a ripple of surprise and irritation passed along the nave. Molly nudged me. 'My parents,' she whispered. I already knew it was them.

The singing began like a thunderclap, with everyone hitting more or less the right note. We sang heartily through an ancient and modern programme, five schools of small children, with the brass section from the secondary modern. Beyond our choir leader I could see all the parents leaning forward, their mouths slightly open, heads lifting and falling with the waves of song, looking bemused, anxious, enraptured. My heart skipped and beat faster.

Molly's solo was coming up. I pinched her arm for good luck. She stayed standing while we all sat down. I could see the back of her head, her ear, the outline of her cheek. Her thin hands hung by her side, limp and still for once, and I had a sudden fear that she wouldn't manage the song. I willed her to sing it right. The hush was immense. It seemed greater during the solos, as though the entire gathering must join forces to keep calamity at bay. Some arched their brows and others lifted their faces and squeezed their eyes shut.

The organ struck a chord and Molly sat out strongly, holding the tune well as it climbed and dipped. Her voice was limpid and sure. 'Glor – or – or – or – or – oria,' she sang 'In excelsis deo. Glor – or – or – or – or . . .'

There was a loud thud at the back of the church, as though a heavy sack had fallen from some height. A long way off, in the aisle at the edge of a pew, I could see Molly's mother on her knees. Her head was hanging down as though it was too heavy for words. Then slowly and with obvious effort she lifted it and seemed to look straight at Molly. She rocked slightly, backwards and forwards, as though she were on a spring that would go on for ever. Then she grabbed the seat and began to pull herself up. Molly's father held her from behind, his face working silently. Heads began to turn away from the altar towards them.

'Leave me!' She pushed him away, staggered and clung to the pew, 'A bleeding angel!' she shouted hoarsely. 'Sings like a bleeding angel!' She lurched and faltered.

Molly looked straight ahead and kept on singing. Her voice was strong as she climbed up and down the dizzy notes. She didn't even turn her head when the vicar flapped down the aisle and circled Molly's parents in his white bat wings. Molly kept on and on singing, eyes to the front where I couldn't see. I saw only the redness creeping up her neck. She wouldn't have seen much anyway. Even I who kept turning to stare, couldn't really see what happened with all the pushing and jostling and shoving Molly's mother to the back and out through the wide squeaking door into the graveyard where our ghosts were probably still flitting around.

The hubbub had died away by the time Molly reached the end of her solo. Our choir leader gave an appreciative nod and the choirs stood and swamped the gloom with song. Molly and I rocked on our feet and sang our lungs out. My eyes were stinging. The familiar tunes and words seemed suddenly thin and insubstantial, unable to carry the choking weight of our singing.

After the concert we were allowed to join our parents if they were there. Molly hung back while my mother fired whispered shots at my ear. 'That woman! And Molly! What a voice! I take my hat off to her!' My mother wasn't wearing a hat.

My father put his arm round Molly who seemed to shrink into him. Then before I realised it, my mother was making arrangements with Miss Rawlings. We were to walk Molly home. She wasn't to worry. My mother would see to it and make sure she was all right. I felt suddenly thankful to my mother, and gratitude rushed up and lodged in my throat.

I caught Molly's arm in the porch. 'The ghosts! Where d'you think they've got to?'

'Oh leave them!' said Molly with dull fury. 'I'm having nothing more to do with that stupid badly behaved creature. We should never have brought them.'

I was troubled. I couldn't bear to think of leaving our ghosts, who were so young and unable to fend for themselves. The place was too cold, and they were hardly more than babies in some ways. What would they do once they were bored of flitting round the gravestones and in and out of the yew? Would they ever find their way back to us in the dark, or would they stay and make mischief in the church, like poltergeists do? It was hard to think of them without us. In my mind they became somehow thinner, more thread-like, in danger of drifting . . . I wasn't sure if they could get angry, even haunt us maybe. I imagined them attaching themselves to us, like tiny fetters. Shivering, I ducked into the wind. 'They can't help it you know,' I said, thinking to mediate between them and Molly. They had no words to help their cause. I understood that much. Molly was silent too, and unrelenting. I asked her what she was thinking. 'Dunno,' she shrugged. I felt the familiar empty ache that I always felt when I realised I'd gone along with her again.

I was glad to have my mother and father close behind us as Molly and I walked hand in hand back across the green. Their wide dark forms seemed to keep the chill off us. The pond, empty of birds, and now covered with a thin film of black ice, was a perfect answering disc to the full moon.

I wondered what would happen when we reached Molly's house. Her sister Jane might open the door and bustle her inside, folding her arms around her and leaving us outside, worrying. How would my mother make sure she was all right? I knew she couldn't really.

Molly suddenly laughed loudly. 'They're back,' she called 'The naughty devils! She clutched at something invisible with her woollen gloved hand, and sure enough I felt a tugging presence at my own sleeve.

'You naughty creature!' I said 'Where did you flit to?'

'Hold hands children! Keep in line! Jack! Pick your feet up!' shrieked Molly as we ran stumbling across the frozen earth in the unfaltering light of the moon.

Christmas Cracker Novelty

June Oldham

Nobody would have known we had done it if Marge hadn't telled. I wouldn't be lying in bed while they're all traipsing off to the chapel fête; you can hear their noise from here so what it must be like in the field is anybody's business. Till Bugler Brown blows it. That soon shuts them up. The first time he does, it'll be the egg and spoon race, they've stuck the list on the gate, so even if Mam changes her mind this minute and says I can go, I shall miss it. She wouldn't let me out till I'd filled the sink and had a wash and she'd brushed my hair, tutting over the cots and taking all day. So Marge has put paid to me getting the prize in the egg and spoon race after all that practising, us lining up at the end of the yard, running to Featherstone's cinder heap and back, then lining up again, till Joan got tired of it and Marge said I was getting so expert no-one could touch me for speed, and everybody dropped at least once. That's what she calls encouragement, whether asked for or not. It comes of her birthday being a year before Joan's and mine, but that's never helped her to think what to play. When I put the spoons back in the dresser, making sure Mam was not in the kitchen, and Joan had slipped the pot eggs under Mrs Bottomley's hedge, which was fair seeing that it was me that had risked borrowing them, all Marge had to suggest was a walk round.

'Round what?' I asked her.

'Round here.' She has a way of pleating her lips so she looks superior. If she feels like that, I don't know why she doesn't go back to where she lived before, except that they were bombed out. That is why she imagines what 'walking round' is smart, like some of them on Sundays, parading their best, but it beat me what Marge thought was the attraction on a Friday after tea when there were only another two and a quarter hours left before bed-time.

Anyway, before I'd had time to say anything, Joan put in, 'I've seen,' and that settled it.

Joan can be like that sometimes; she'll dig her heels in and a steam roller won't shift her. Mam says the Templemans have been like that from time immemorial. Mind you, you can get round them if you try hard enough; it's a question of going about it the right way. If Marge had said, 'Race you to the church and back,' Joan would have been up like a shot.

After Joan had stated her opinion, Marge looked as if she might go back to her house and that would have left just two which isn't much use. Three is better for playing despite what they say about two's company and three's none, because you always need one to keep cave. So I had to think fast.

If I had known what would happen, I'd have said, 'Since you want a walk round, you go on, Marge. All you have to do is take a step up Main Street, then saunter down the path past the Wesleyan till you get to Four Lanes' End, struggle over the bridge, and you're back top of Main Street. If you take your time, you can do it easy before the five to six bus comes.' The church clock was striking quarter to when I should have been saying it. Only I didn't. I haven't any time for people who are sarky; I have enough of that with Mrs Croft at school. But if I had said it and Marge had taken the huff and left me and Joan, I wouldn't be here now, in bed and not allowed to go to the fête. It's my mam's favourite punishment, sending me to bed to wait for dad's verdict, and that won't be the strap, like it is with Joan's dad which gets it over quick; instead our dad likes to think up different ideas such as mucking out the pig or going without tea. 'And you take your shoes off and get right into that bed,' Mam said; 'I'm not having you lolling out of the window exchanging the time of day with all the world as they go past.'

If I had said that remark to Marge, and she had flounced off, I wouldn't have had to knock on my brains to know what we could do. I wouldn't have run into our kitchen and fished in the biscuit barrel on the dresser where I'd dropped it after Christmas under the identity discs, my sweet coupons and some three ha'penny stamps. I wouldn't have taken it into the shed and shown them.

'Got it in a Christmas cracker,' I said.

'Which Christmas?' Marge asked. It was like her to be suspicious. 'Crackers have gone off the market.'

They have not gone off the market my uncle Trim visits, and neither has tinned salmon, but I didn't mention that. 'Can't remember,' I answered, 'but I expect it's been about quite a bit.'

Joan wasn't interested in Marge's question. On or off the market, crackers never find their way to the Templeman's table. Mr Templeman has what the vicar calls a full quiver, by which he seems to mean too many children. Joan is the middle one so far. She asked, 'What's it supposed to be?'

'There were instructions came with it,' I told her. 'They said it was for telling whether a person's a man or a woman.'

Joan was puzzled, I could see that, but she wasn't going to show it. 'I know who's a man or a woman without putting the question to that!' she answered.

'What if one of them's in disguise?' I asked her.

Joan snorted. 'Who in Little Swinham puts on disguises? If they did, we'd soon find out, wouldn't we? We'd miss who they were before.'

'Let's have a look,' Marge said, so I handed her the cracker novelty.

It was made of tin and a bit shorter than my little finger and about as thick as a pipe cleaner, only hollow inside like a tube. There was a hole punched in one end and a piece of red silk threaded through it. Marge tried to blow down the middle without touching it with her mouth; she is faddy about dirt.

'It's not a whistle,' I reminded her. 'It's an implement for deciding sex.'

Marge blushed. 'I wish you'd stop being rude.'

'It's not me that's rude; it's them that wrote it on the paper inside the cracker that's rude. Handy Sex Diviner they call it.'

That made Marge blush even more and she gave me the diviner back quick, saying, 'That's dirty.'

I should have put it away and not said any more. I should have remembered the last time that sex had been giving an airing. I had ended up in bed, same as now, only it wasn't the fête I could hear in Mumby's field but Charlie Wells from next door shouting about his new bike that had been Billy Foley's and I could have a turn if I wanted. And it was Marge's fault then as much as it is now, except that she didn't clat, not in so many words. That time, it was by the way she looked that Mam suspected.

I had pointed out to Marge she could go back home if she felt like that, but she didn't. She hung about outside the shed and kept putting her head in, whining about what would happen to me and Joan if we was caught, and leaving the door open a crack so she could gleg at a safe distance. She even had the face to pass comment, saying that me and Joan looked ridiculous, and when I pointed out that her mam and dad must have done it at least twice since their wedding, she said it was none of my business but she could not imagine them behaving like stupids.

'You mean they do it like Holme's stallion?' Joan asked, a bit out of breath from the way I was squashing her.

'I mean they do it in a decent fashion at night when we're asleep,' Marge retorted, not answering Joan's question.

'Well, my dad grunts; you can hear him all over the house,' Joan said. Then she complained that the truss of straw we was propped against was pricking her bottom. So she insisted on changing places and started to grunt and rub her wee hole against mine like mad. Only she was not long changing her noise because after a bit with the heat and the tickle, we were both squeaking.

'If you want babies you need a man with a thing,' she said.

'That's all right. You don't have to apologise,' I told her. 'Mothers don't have them all the time so perhaps they rub. I reckon I wouldn't mind that.'

Joan nodded. 'So long as you don't get sore.' She spat on her palm and dabbed.

'Have you finished now?' Marge demanded.

'Oh, go and take a run,' Joan whipped out. 'You're frit.'

'I'm not. I don't know what you think you gain from trying an experiment, as Lena calls it, when it's only you two.'

'If you like, I'll fetch Charlie Wells. I expect he'd let you try it on him. He'd not be averse to having a go.'

'You keep me out of it,' Marge had answered and backed from the door, blushing.

When Mam came to fasten up the clothes line, she could not help but notice Marge stood by the wall under the hook, and being our mam she immediately got wind of our doings by the panicky look in Marge's face and her eyes rolling round. The first thing I knew was a slap, and then it was orders to bed and wait till Dad heard. I blamed Marge for that but it was more chance that I'd made Joan swap places again. You could not do it with your knickers up and and when Mam laid on she fetched up a real smart. She hasn't half got a hand on her when it comes to slapping.

If I had remembered that time I had been sent up here to bed, I might have taken the Sex Diviner back into the kitchen and dropped it into the biscuit barrel where it belonged, but I'd forgotten; and in any case, trying to work out what people do when they are married and a gadget for deciding their sex didn't in my mind have much connection. I'd have expected they were clear on that point before they started up. So it is a funny thing that I didn't think of Mrs Featherstone straight off.

'I've never seen anything like that,' Joan said, having a good squint. 'My dad hasn't got one, and him and Arthur can tell in less than no time, even new born chicks.'

'Not everybody lives on a farm,' I argued generously. 'There must be people about who aren't so sharp. Else they wouldn't have put this in a cracker.'

'Can you tell if a chicken's a cockerel or a hen?' Joan asked Marge. She wasn't intending to provoke her, just check, but Marge took the question the wrong way.

'Of course I can't,' she snapped. 'I don't need to. But I can tell the difference between a man and a woman and I don't have to go looking inside a Christmas cracker for something to teach me. I reckon I can see whether it's a man or woman without a silly tube on a string.'

'What about Mrs Featherstone?' I asked.

That shut her up.

I suppose we must get back to Mrs Featherstone about once a week, but we never get tired of her. There's always her head to talk about because now and again one of us will think she's seen a few hairs showing round the edge of her cap, the same one, day in and day out, that fits tight all over and she crocheted herself. If there are any hairs, then Joan's wrong and I'm half right and Marge has won, because Joan reckons Mrs Featherstone's head is entirely bald; I imagine she's probably got a big empty patch on the top; and Marge, who thinks that all old women should be grandmas like hers who would not budge despite the air raids, insists that under Mrs Featherstone's cap is a mass of grey speckled curls. I would do anything to find out the truth. When she took ill once I offered to go round with the blancmange Mam had made, expecting she would have the cap off in bed, but she hadn't. Marge said that served me right for being such a hypocrite but I told her that she wouldn't be saying that if Mrs Featherstone's hat had been off and her head was covered instead with tight little curls. At times it strikes me that Marge would rather not know, because what is found out might not be what she hopes for, whereas I don't mind whose notion is the right one so long as it is proved. She refused to stand cave and ran home when I said all that was needed was for me and Joan to get up on the shed and fish for the cap with a rake as soon as Mrs Featherstone passed, so we couldn't do it; if Mam had lit on us without warning, it would have been bed for a week. Marge won't even allow that Mrs Featherstone has got whiskers, saying it's fluff on her face off a towel. Me and Joan say it's not, but we can never get close enough to be sure because every time Mrs Featherstone comes to the pump, she shoos us off, and she'd got the blinds drawn when I took the blancmange. Then there's her washing. She pegs it out every Monday across the grass at the end of the yard alongside Charlie Wells's mam's line. But mostly she's standing guard when I come home to dinner and she's taken it in by the end of the afternoon school, so it's a hard job to get a peek. Now and again I've managed it, though, and it seems that either Mr Featherstone changes some other time as well as bath night, or they both wear the same, because there are two pairs of long combinations. There are never any bloomers. As I say to Joan, if she wears combinations all week, you'd expect her to have bloomers for church. Even Joan's dad doesn't wear his workaday shirt on Sunday. So there's another puzzle, and they all add up to one thing: there's a good chance that Mrs Featherstone is a man. When I stood in the shed holding the Sex Diviner, it came to me that at last I had a way of putting paid to arguments.

'That's a horrid thing to do.' Marge said.

'You come up with something better.'

'I don't want to. As far as I'm concerned, she's just an old lady.'

'If she is, you shouldn't be afraid of giving her a test.'

In the normal course of events I can't talk as crafty. So it must have been the cracker novelty gave me the inspiration. I was pleased with the words that came out and Marge saw. She didn't half glare.

'You're growing too big for your boots, Lena Appleyard, especially in Little Swinham.' She likes having a dig at the village when she can, though she hadn't said no when Mrs Cook took the whole family in. 'Anyway, what makes you think it will work?'

'It does. I've tried it. You just look.' I grabbed Joan's hand and held the Sex Diviner above it. You have to grip the red tag between finger and thumb and wait. It wasn't more than a second before the metal tube gave a jump and went round in circles. 'See,' I crowed. 'That means she's female.'

'As if we don't know!' Marge said.

'It's *it* knowing that matters, you fathead,' Joan told her. 'Let's have a proper see, Lena. How does it work?' She was growing excited, which is saying a lot when you bear in mind she is one of the Templemans. But after she had licked it and given it a thorough sniff, she said, 'I give up. I expect our Arthur would have the answer. He's a dab hand with the Ferguson.'

'It's no mystery,' Marge insisted. 'If you let it hang like that, it's sure to go round and round. I can't see what that's got to do with anyone being a female.'

'Because it doesn't do that for a man,' I told her. 'It swings from side to side like a pendulum.'

'Show me!'

'Who with?' We all looked out of the shed; there wasn't a man in sight. Most times that is a relief because if they are there they are forever chasing you off their gardens and never miss an opportunity to come round to the back door and put in a complaint. 'Don't you suggest Charlie Wells,' I forestalled her as he ran across to their lav. 'I wouldn't play with him if he paid me.'

'It's not so much playing with him as asking a favour,' Joan pointed out. She can be clever when she wants.

I did not like the way Marge was quiet; she had a smug look on her and it occurred to me that I had to check that the Diviner still 'Responded to the male aura' - that is what was written on the instructions - like it had at Christmas, because if something had gone wrong with it, it would go in circles for Mrs Featherstone as well, not showing that she was a man.

'You don't need a man on the spot,' I came up with, glad that I had remembered what it said on the instructions. 'You can do it with any old thing that belongs to him.'

Again, there was not a single bit of anything around like that, not that we could see. Even Marge was disappointed. 'And they spend their time dropping articles for everyone else to pick up!' she tutted, sounding like her mother.

At last Joan solved the problem. 'Here,' she said, 'I forgot. This is Arthur's old scarf. He let me have it when Mam knitted him a new one,' and she laid it out on the shed floor.

I was nervous with Marge standing, ready to be sarky, and I didn't like the way the Diviner seemed undecided at first. It was as if it wanted to go round, but as Joan pointed out, since she had worn the scarf last, not Arthur, there could be confusion. 'It'll right itself in a minute,' she assured me; 'when it's cottoned on.' And of course it did. Soon, with me pinching the loop of silk tightly, the tin tube was swinging twenty to the dozen.

Not one of us said anything; you could have heard a pin drop. I was convinced it was magic but I was not going to mention that: Joan had superstitions and Marge would have thought herself called upon to jeer, being a year older. So I just let the Diviner swing. After a minute or two, to show her that the Diviner Operator – like it said in the cracker – did not have to be anyone special, I asked Marge if she would like a go, but she jumped back, declaring she didn't want it anywhere near her. But when it came to plans she had no bones about joining in them. One minute she's criticising, the next she's all for it as much as me and Joan. You don't know where you are with her nowadays. She was not like this first off when she came to play.

It was a bit before we decided on the lav. Anything else we could think of was beyond us. The only one who had a chance of getting Mrs Featherstone to hold out her hand under the Diviner was Marge, and she would not countenance that. None of us could wait till Monday to put it to any of Mrs Featherstone's washing, and in any case we didn't know which pair of combinations was hers. We considered the piece of matting she kneels on when she scrubs her causey, to cushion her knees against the bricks, but since I borrowed it once to make a seat across Charlie Wells's cross-bar, she's always kept it in sight when she swills out the bucket and sticks it in her wash-house straight after. So, in the end, we had no choice. We had to dangle the Sex Diviner over the seat of her lav.

There was no difficult about knowing when she had visited; all we had to was sit with the shed door open and watch till she ran down her causey and across the yard. It was getting in after that was the stumbling block. We did not expect Mr Froggatt at the end would show any interest; he keeps to himself and if he saw us going into one of the lavs, it was not likely he would count along the row and say to hisself: those little monkeys should not be using number three. Or if he did see, he would not be bothered. He told me once that provided we kept our ball out of his garden, he did not care a cuss where it went. But that left Charlie Well's mother and our mam who could see us, besides Mrs Featherstone. And all the husbands, including our dad; except they were bringing in the hay.

There was no way of doing it without risks. As soon as Mrs Featherstone had been and was back in her kitchen, two of us had to walk by the lavs, past the Wells' as if going into ours, but one had to sidle into the next lav instead. There did not seem any point in dipping for who was working the Sex Diviner since it was mine. Joan was the one to go with me, and Marge to keep cave.

We should have kept her out of it. We should have decided that Joan should come out of our lav and keep watch. We should have left Marge to wait in the shed, or 'walk round' or something. But we did not. So I'm missing the chapel fête. I would be there now, winning the egg and spoon race, if it had not been for Marge. I should never have trusted her. You would not find one of the Templemans blabbing.

And Marge might not have gone clatting if there had not been the blood. Or if Joan had been there when I told her. Everything had gone smoothly up to then. I had a few bad moments when I heard steps but it was only Mr Froggatt whose lav is next to the Featherstones', and when he was installed I had to ram my hanky in my mouth to stifle the giggles. What with the groans and swearing and his feet drumming, he was putting more effort into it than he has ever given to his garden or pumping up his bike tyres. Listening to him, I had a job with the Diviner. First it nearly dropped down the hole, then I could not keep my hand still, so it went all ways except swing. I got it under control, though, after Joan hissed to hear what it was doing, and it was soon going like clockwork, backwards and forwards, as lively as you could wish. I told Joan through the wall and she said she would go out, giving me a whistle if nobody was there. We were all back in the shed inside three minutes.

It should have been the moment to celebrate. At last, we were sure. But Joan said the result did not surprise her and Marge looked as though she was going to cry, and I had the other thing to tell them which was as important as Mrs Featherstone being a man. I gave myself time to wrap my hanky round the Sex Diviner and hide it behind the straw trusses and was closing the shed door so that no one would hear, when Joan's Arthur shouted from the end of the yard that she was wanted. Hearing him rev up the tractor, she was off, begging a ride.

That left me and Marge, her snivelling and me blown up with news. I should have waited. I should have said to myself: Better wait till tomorrow; Joan will want to be in on it from the start. Better wait till tomorrow and tell them both at the chapel fête. Only I did not.

'Marge,' I said, 'shall I tell you what I saw in Featherstones' lav?'

'No, thanks,' she said, making a show of dabbing her eyes. 'I don't want to know. But I'll bet anything you can name that it's disgusting. It always is, when you've made it up. I don't believe that Diviner. It's a trick. Mrs Featherstone is a gentle old lady, like my gran.'

'Have you seen her shift the piano in the church room?' I interrupted.

Marge took no notice. 'I don't see why you cannot leave her alone. How would you like it if someone followed you to the lav and waggled a gadget over the seat and then said you weren't a girl?'

'She doesn't know.'

'Maybe she already guesses, the way you and Joan study her. But I don't reckon it matters whether she does or not. The fact remains you've done it.'

That was too deep for me and I was not going to be stopped by it. If I did not get my news out soon, I would choke. 'That Sex Diviner has just proved Mrs Featherstone is a man for certain,' I told her, 'but that's not all I found out in their lav. There is something else. What I saw. There's blood all over the paper down the hole. Sheets and sheets of it, covered.'

'You shouldn't have looked,' she gasped out.

'I don't go deliberately poking my nose down people's dirt closets! When you are operating a Sex Diviner above a lav seat you can't have your eyes closed. So I saw.'

'If you can't keep your eyes closed, at least pay attention to your mouth,' she answered, her face going white.

'But it's important. She, he, is trying to hide blood.'

'You shouldn't talk about it.' She squatted down on the shed floor and stuffed her hands between her legs.

'I'm not talking about it, I'm just telling you. You don't keep quiet when someone next door to you is trying to get rid of blood.'

'She's an old woman,' Marge insisted, hiding her eyes in her hanky. 'She must be near forty if she's a day. She can't help it when she gets ill.'

'She's as fit as a fiddle. She took a full row of new spuds up last week and bagged them for our mam.' Then I remembered. 'She's a man, anyway, and he has done something.' I could not spit it out; my thoughts were moving too fast for the words.

'What do you mean, done something? You don't do it. It happens.'

I was not to be put off by quibbles. 'And now he's trying to cover it up.'

'You're off your rocker.' Her face was like the ash from under the cinders and she was writhing about, her fingers kneading her tummy. 'Nobody wants it seen.'

'Of course they don't, that's why the hole was full of it, and even the squares of paper cut up from the Echo that were still hanging from the string had bloody finger marks stuck on them. We'll have to go back for those, Marge; they'll be needed.' I was not offering to do any sieving. When they heard, the authorities could do that themselves.

But Marge would not even agree to rescuing the fingerprints. She jumped up, giving a sort of bleat, and ran out.

After that, there was not much I could do. I could not go in the Featherstones' lav every time she, he, ran across, not without Joan and Marge giving assistance. So I could only keep watch, getting in some more practice for the race, except I had to use a pebble. Charlie Wells had come out with the warning that Mrs Bottomley had been round to their house grumbling about her pot eggs, so it was only a matter of time before the penny dropped and she was complaining to our mam. She has not done yet, but when she starts on it, there'll be no excuse to soften her; I shan't be able to tell her I won.

I would have had a fighting chance if I had been let. I would be there now, running this very minute – Bugler Brown's just let rip – if there had not been ructions before dinner, Marge's mam arriving and asking to speak to our mam in private and then our mam dragging me upstairs. She has got a terrible grip. She said I deserve all the punishment that will be meted out and the cracker novelty was going on the back of the fire and it was about time I could find something useful to occupy myself with instead of poking my nose into other folk's business and the devil finds work for idle hands.

When she had calmed down a bit, she said I could chase the silly ideas out of my head, but there were explanations and I would be told in due course.

Well, I've thought about them long enough but none of them is without some puzzle. Mrs Featherstone being a man would explain why they haven't any children and I expect instead of making babies they just rub, but how could the proper Mr Featherstone have made the mistake of choosing in the first place? Most people manage without a Sex Diviner. And what about if there is not a proper Mr Featherstone at all, but the one we call Mrs Featherstone acts for them both and it took the Sex Diviner to see through the disguises? I bet our mam never thought of that. On the other hand, say she's right and Mrs Featherstone is a woman the same as the others, what is she doing messing about with all that blood?

The fact is, when Mam said there were explanations and I would be told in due course, she wasn't denying there is a mystery.

I'm waiting to hear it.

Contributors' Notes

Malorie Blackman is an ex-computer programmer who now writes full time. *Not So Stupid*! her first collection of short stories (Livewire Books for Teenagers, The Women's Press, 1990), was a Selected Title for Feminist Book Fortnight, 1991. Since then she has published over a dozen books, including *Hacker* (Doubleday Books/Corgi Books) and the *Girl Wonder* series (Victor Gollancz/ Puffin Books) and has contributed to numerous anthologies. She lives in London, and her latest novel, *Trust Me*, has recently been published by Livewire Books For Teenagers, The Women's Press.

Petronella Breinburg is originally from Surinam in the West Indies and is best known for her children's books and academic papers. She has also published a number of short stories and had plays produced in fringe theatres. At present she is a senior lecturer in the English department of Goldsmiths' College, London University, and has just returned from reading her poetry and talking about her writing in Austria and Finland.

Glyn Brown is a freelance journalist whose work has appeared in the *Guardian, TLS, City Limits, i–D*, and more. She won the 1991 *Time Out* short story competition and other fiction has appeared in *The Word Party* (Centre for Creative and Peforming Arts), *The Plot Against Mary* (The Women's Press, 1992), *New Writing 2* (Minerva) and *Time Out's Book of London Short Stories* (Penguin). She is currently completing her first novel, *The Fabulous Wild*. She lives in a dream world, just off the Lea Bridge roundabout.

Alison Campbell is co-editor of this anthology. She has two children and lives in London. She works with children and young adults.

Maude Casey was born in England to Irish parents, and she enjoys the richness of her two cultural backgrounds. Her first novel, *Over the Water* (Livewire Books for Teenagers, The Women's Press, 1987), was shortlisted for the Whitbread Literary Award and the Fawcett Book Prize. She is currently working on a collection of short fiction and her second novel, for which she has received an Arts Council Bursary. She lives in Brighton with her two children and their father.

Mary Ciechanowska lives in London, has done a lot of teaching, helped produce a fair amount of non-fiction, written several short stories and a little pyre of chapter ones.

Eleanor Dare is behind the controversial *How To* books – *How To Fly Light Aircraft* and *How To Rewire Your House* created by cutting up texts and rearranging them at random.

Helen Dunmore has published four collections of poems, all from Bloodaxe Books, two novels for young people and a novel, *Zennor in Darkness* (Viking, 1992). Her short stories have appeared in magazines and anthologies.

Sylvia Fair was born in Rhayader, a small market town in mid-Wales, daughter of a dispensing chemist. She has three sons and two daughters. She began writing seriously when they were very young. Her first novel, *The Ivory Anvil* (Gollancz), was selected runner-up for the 1974 Guardian Children's Fiction Award, and was produced on BBC's *Jackanory*. She writes and illustrates picture books for younger children too. She has recently completed an adult novel. Her short stories have been anthologised in an Arts Council/PEN publication, and she has also broadcast on *Morning Story*. She writes poetry under the name of Sylvia Turner and was placed runner-up in 1990 in both the National Poetry Competition and the Arvon International. In 1991, she was runner-up in the Skoob International. She lives in London with her husband Bill Turner, poet.

Caroline Hallett is co-editor of this and the previous two seasonal collections. She works with young people in North London and lives with her partner and young children just north of London. She writes mainly on the train between work and home and is travelling, hopefully, towards a collection of her own stories.

Susan King was born in Birkenhead in 1952. She left school when she was sixteen but returned to full-time education ten years later to take a degree in Sociology at Salford University. She now lives in North London and divides her time between lecturing and writing. 'Gastric Measures' won first prize at the Southampton University 12th Annual Writers Conference. She is currently working on her first novel and co-editing an anthology of short stories by women on the theme of horror.

Shena Mackay was born in Edinburgh in 1944 and grew up in Kent and London, where she now lives. Her work includes the novellas *Toddler on the Run* and *Dust Falls on Eugene Schlumberger*, published when she was twenty, *Music Upstairs* (1965), *Old Crow* (1967), *An Advent Calendar* (1971), *Babies in Rhinestones* (1983), *A Bowl of Cherries* (1984), *Redhill Rococo* (1986) – which won the Fawcett Prize – *Dreams of Dead Women's Handbags* (1987), *Dunedin* (1992) and *The Laughing Academy* (1993). She has also written a play for the National Theatre, *Nurse Macater*, and regularly writes stories for the BBC and others.

Moy McCrory has published three collections of short stories and a novel, *The Fading Shrine* (Jonathan Cape). More recently she wrote two stage commissions for youth theatre. She writes a weekly review for *The Times* and is working on a second novel. She is an occasional lecturer at Goldsmiths' where she tutors the creative writing course. She lives with her husband, their two young children and an elderly cat.

June Oldham writes for all ages. Adult novels are *A Little Rattle in the Air* and *Flames* which received a prize (Virago). Among her novels for adolescents are *Grow Up, Cupid* and *Double Take*. Her short stories have appeared in *Strand, Panurge*, and several anthologies. Between books she has directed the Ilkley Literature Festival, held writing residencies, and she undertakes workshops, talks and readings.

Jenny Palmer teaches EAP to postgraduate students at King's and Goldsmiths' colleges. She has been writing and publishing since 1985, both journalistic and creative work. She lives in Hackney, but is proud of and draws inspiration from her Northern upbringing. She is currently researching and working on her third novel about a witch, who she likes to think of as a long-lost ancestor. She is a founder member of the collective who put together *The Man Who Loved Presents* and *The Plot Against Mary*, and co-editor of this anthology.

Gerda (GA) Pickin was born in Oakland, California in 1952. She qualified as an archaeologist, and became a British citizen in 1979. She is currently living in Co Durham with her partner and twin daughters.

Tara Rimsk writes poetry and fiction. Her story 'ACDC' was published in *Wild Hearts*, the first anthology of contemporary lesbian melodrama to appear in Britain (Sheba, 1991). A short story, 'The Moonboat', is being published this autumn by Onlywomen Press in their anthology, *Unknown Territory*. She is also co-editing a collection of short stories as well as continuing to write her own.

Daphne Schiller read English at Manchester University and later obtained an MA in Creative Writing at the University of East Anglia. She has taught in schools and colleges, and is at present working for the WEA. Her poetry has been published in several magazines and broadcast on radio and TV. She is now working on a collection of short stories.

Marijke Woolsey has produced three novels, the first was short-listed for the Betty Trask Award, and the third is with her agent. She has also produced many short stories, some of which have been published. She has two children. She teaches creative writing at a Hammersmith and Fulham Adult Education College. She is co-editor of *The Man Who Loved Presents*, *The Plot Against Mary* and . . . *And a Happy New Year*!

Zhana is a writer, singer and personal growth consultant. Two other short stories of hers, 'Unto Us' and 'The Gift', have been published in previous The Women's Press anthologies, *The Man Who Loved Presents* and *The Plot Against Mary*. She is currently working on a science fiction novelette, 'The Babymaker', and a choreopoem, 'Dance of the Warrior'. 'Home for Christmas' is an exerpt from her novel-in-progress, *The Treasures of Darkness*.

Also of interest:

Campbell, Hallett, Palmer, Woolsey, eds
The Man Who Loved Presents
and
The Plot Against Mary

The two bestselling predecessors to . . . *And a Happy New Year!*
Powerful antidotes to standard seasonal fare, these sparkling
stories take more irreverent looks at this 'happy family time'.

Fiction £6.99
ISBN 0 7043 4289 8 (*The Man Who Loved Presents*)
ISBN 0 7043 4328 2 (*The Plot Against Mary*)